KASAK

CRAZE OF A WOMAN FOR UNFILLED DESIRE

K. RAM

PARTRIDGE

A Penguin Random House Company

To order additional copies of this book, contact
Toll Free 800 101 2657 (Singapore)
Toll Free 1 800 81 7340 (Malaysia)
orders.singapore@partridgepublishing.com

www.partridgepublishing.com/singapore

PREFACE

H E WAS HAPPY AND CHEERFUL on this assignment. He decided to accept the job and then kids can be called during vacation. He joined and was happy with his job. He was very friendly and open hearted person. He helped the people out of the way.

He was of helping nature without shyness. It was very difficult situation when he helped one of the co-passengers. She fell sick on the way while in transit in a hotel. She was unable to go out for anything. He arranged all facility, amenity from the hotel administration and medicine for her. His behavior was noticed by co-passenger.

He was in mid thirties, young and handsome. He does all his work cheerfully. After joining the work, he solved existing problem at work. Soon he became popular in his department. This is a small country and most of the people know each other. So he became famous soon among locals. Some of the local girls tried to trap him but were un-successful.

If you can't defeat your enemy, you can win him by becoming his friend. Then you can do everything. This idea was utilized and ultimately he was trapped. Further what had happened read in this book. Hope you would also had done the same in the similar situation like person in this book.

This is true story. It is about what had happened with a person while he was on foreign assignment. Texts in parentheses "xx" are the verse of Sandra. Texts without parentheses are his.

K. Ram

[🕴]

TELEPHONE WAS RINGING. I RUSHED out from bedroom to take the phone which was kept in the hall. I lifted the phone and said—Hello!

No response from other side. I said again Hello—hello! No response from other side.

I was about to hang then got response in sweet voice.

"Hello, Hello! This is me."

Who is there?

"Guess who!"

I am not able to guess. Please tell me who you are.

"I am Sandra. Hope you know me now and you may recognise me".

Yes, now I know you. Why you remain silent on phone? I was calling hello-hello.

"It seems some problem in my phone."

I see. This is your first phone call that's why I could not recognise your voice.

"Well hope next time I have not to tell you my name."

No, of course not, I can recognise your voice on phone now.

"I want to meet you can I come?"

Yes, of course, you may come.

"I want to meet you right now"

Well what is time now?

"It is exactly six in the evening. Are you still sleeping?"

No, you wake me up now. Give me half hour for fresh up.

"Sounds good to me"

This was pleasant evening. Cool breeze was blowing. The time was for evening tea. I got fresh and started preparing tea. Sweet and salty biscuit was kept on the table. Sister Sandra was not late. She was staying just 100 meter away from my flat. I know her personally. We started foreign journey together in the same flight. She appreciated my help all the way and during stay at transit. I heard knock at door. I open door found Sandra was standing with a small bag in her hand.

Welcome Sister Sandra.

"Thank you. Please call me Sandra. Don't call Sister Sandra. Just Sandra would be fine."

All right I'll address you Sandra now.

"It sounds good to me. What are you doing?"

I am preparing tea.

"Tea for me?"

Yes for both of us.

"I like coffee not tea."

Sorry, Sandra I am having only tea. Hope you won't mind. Take tea this time next time you will get coffee. I shall keep coffee in home. Please taste tea prepared by me.

I offered her biscuits mean while and brought cups of tea on the table. I gave one to her. She sipped tea.

"Oh! Very nice tea I like this. How have you prepared?"

Take required amount of water, add a pinch of fresh crushed ginger and boiled it. Then add tea leaves in it and later add milk and wait till it boiled again. Now filter the tea and add sugar as per taste. I generally add more milk in the tea. Ratio of water and milk in the tea is fifty—fifty.

"That's why it is so tasty."

Thanks for compliments. You liked it otherwise I was thinking to offer juice or milk. I feel really sorry for not having coffee in the house.

"Never mind, this tea is much better than coffee."

My pleasure—I replied.

"What you are doing in the evening?"

I'll go for evening walk and back home.

"Every day you go for walk."

Yes, walk is good for health and passing time also.

"That is right. Can I take some time of your and talk to you?"

Yes, Why not. Please go ahead.

"I heard news about you when you shifted in this flat from hotel?"

I shifted from hotel in this flat a month ago. I had stayed just for fifteen days in this flat when an incident took place. You know this is only occupied flat in this row other flats are abandoned.

"Yes I know. My flat is nearby just hundred meters away from yours. Tell me what had happened?"

Leave that Sandra, don't remind me.

"So you do not want to tell me."

You have already heard it.

"I want to know from you."

Well, it was Friday evening I back from my evening walk. I took a glass of water with lime juice and then had rest. It was 8:30 in the evening. I took bath sit for prayer. I enjoyed a cup of tea. I started cooking at half pass nine.

I cooked lentil soup, rice, vegetable and prepared chapattis (bread). You know I have to keep some soup and vegetable for lunch. In the lunch I warm it and bake fresh chapattis only. Thus I save time and take little rest during lunch.

It was eleven in the night. I finished my dinner. I warmed a cup of milk and enjoying it on the dining table. I heard knock at the door. I rushed to door and moved curtain little but no one was there. I have been told that lizard's also making sound similar of knock on the door. So I thought it may be lizard. I back to seat. Second time again I heard knock opened curtain but no one.

Third time again sound came. This time I thought will open door and go out to see what is happening. I removed curtain and found an unknown girl standing near coconut tree showing her private part by covering her face. I pulled curtain back immediately. I took cup of milk and gone in the bedroom. I finished milk and came to put cup in the tub. I came back in dining hall and found she is knocking and showing her private part to me. I informed my neighbour opposite side flat for help. He called police.

At one o'clock Police came for search. He could not find any one there. Police knocked my door and asked me to look for the girl troubling you.

I came out of the house and look around but could not find anyone. Next morning I told this incident to local staff in my office. Local guys believe it was ghost. They advised me not to open door if happened again. I was fearful few days before back to normal.

"Yes I heard this story but was more spicy"

What spicy?

"Rumour is that you are impotent. Local girls visits places where handsome guys, like you, staying alone. They want to enjoy night life. They need drink, share dinner and enjoy whole the night. I was told by my local staff working with me."

I can't do that. How they expect I will spend night with stranger?

"Tell that man he is stupid and shown his stupidity by calling Police—Sandra told me in her friends wording."

You know her. Who was she? I asked her.

"She is one of staff from hospital."

I can't do this with anyone. I shall go for evening walk now.

"You can't go for walk today."

Why not?

"It is raining outside"

I open door curtain and saw rain. We both laughed.

I asked her if she like another cup of tea. Sandra agreed.

"I shall wash cups for you and let me prepare tea as you told me"

She washed cups and vessel for tea.

"Let me start making tea, you guide me."

Ok. You can start. Here is tea, sugar and ginger. Milk is kept in fridge.

I guided her and she prepared tea. Tea was tasty. She was happy that tea comes out with good flavour.

"Now I learned one recipe from you to make good and tasty tea. This will help me not to depend on coffee."

You should take coffee. It gives different taste and flavour. Now it was half pass seven in the evening. It was still raining outside.

"Why you worry so much? Tomorrow is Sunday, holiday for you. Let it rain."

I cannot stop rain even I want also.

"You must invite me for dinner. I heard you are very good in cooking too."

You are welcome sister.

"Why you are calling me sister again? This is home not hospital. Call me by my name please."

Sorry I'll call you by name. We chitchat for some time and passed time.

"May I prepare dinner for you?"

No I'll cook dinner today.

"Then start cooking. It is half pass eight now. I shall assist you as helper."

I took out eggplant, potatoes, spinach, and chilli from shelf and started chopping. She was watching me how I am preparing for cooking dinner.

I washed peeled potatoes, spinach and kept aside for draining. I pealed onion, garlic and fine chopped it. I washed tomatoes make its pieces. Chilli was fine chopped too. I chopped potatoes and spinach and kept aside.

I put cooking oil in frying pan on electric stove and switched on at low heat. Oil got heated then added some cumin seeds, later chopped garlic, chilli and onion in to frying pan. Stir it till onion became golden brown. Now added chopped potatoes, spinach and egg plant covered it to steam.

Next added spices, (turmeric power, coriander power and clove, bay leave powers etc.) and salt to taste. Covered frying pan with its lid and after 15 minutes chopped coriander leaves were added and stirred, covered it with frying pan lid. Vegetable was ready in few minutes.

I cooked rice in rice cooker. Taken required amount of rice washed it and kept in cooker, added required amount of water and then switched power on. Rice was cooked in 30 minutes.

I mixed wheat flour, a pinch of salt and water. Kneaded flour till it became ready for baking bread. Prepared bread and apply little butter milk over it.

I gave her Coca-Cola to drink while I was cooking. Rain was slow but not stopped. It was ten o'clock and dinner was ready. We started dinner.

"Food is really very tasty. I am enjoying dinner. My husband also cooks tasty food like you."

Dinner was over. I take warm milk after dinner so I asked her if she likes.

"Yes, I will take and enjoy whatever you like to take. Today I'll not say no for anything."

I warmed two glass of milk in microwave. I gave one to her and sat of sofa sipping hot milk.

It was eleven in night. I feel sleepy. I asked if she can go to her flat.

"No I want to pass evening with you."

That's right we have enjoyed evening. Now it is late in night you must go to your flat and rest.

"I did night duty and I have off tomorrow. I want to spend tonight here. It is raining heavy outside."

I got scared. No, sister you must go to your flat now.

"Look at my clothes I put worn old and it is torn many places. Let us enjoy otherwise I'll tell everyone that you are forcing me to have sex."

I have never asked you did me?

"She tears off her clothes two three places and asked me shall I go out and tell that you have done it?"

I was silent. What to do in this situation.

"Think if I go out like this. You will be defamed and removed from service."

But I have not done this.

"Who believe you after seeing me in this cloth?"

In fact I was young and of her age. All other who came with us on foreign assignment were retired and old. I gain lot more respect among them. I came forward as leader when our plane was defective and police did not allowed us to go out and rest in the hotel.

I came forward and asked air line ground staff to provide us comfortable place to stay. How long we'll sit in transit lounge? Finally ground staff contacted police officials and took us escorted to hotel where we stayed two nights. I helped all the co-passenger in the hotel also.

Sister Maria was travelling with us fell sick in the hotel. I arranged room services for her and Sandra as both sharing same room. I arranged medicine for Maria. This I did when Sandra requested me.

I was in problem now. I requested her you are my sister. Please go to your flat and leave me alone.

"Every women is sister of someone, girlfriend and wife of others. Do you agree or not. I told you in the beginning please call me by my name. Do not call sister"

That is your thinking. You are still sister to me. Rain started heavily. It appears rain was not going to stop.

"See God wants the same what I want. You are really foolish. Why you want to spoil your reputation among your friends? If I phone to police and tell them you are forcing me. You will be taken under custody and asked to leave the country, every one come to know the reason. They all will hate you."

It was midnight both the side I am fixed. If I refused she will defame me. If accept I will be demoralized inside. I was thinking some way to get rid off from this situation.

She switched off all light and holds me in her arms. She was so excited and seduced me too. She forced me in the bed and we both ejaculated. Our clothes were wet with semen.

"What you have done? Without putting inside you fell off (ejaculated). She my clothes got wet. You make me wet."

She removed her clothes and forced me to lie down in bed. She was nude. I pushed her aside and came out of the bedroom. She tore her dress and threatens me of the consequences.

I requested her to spare me but she never listen to me. She took telephone twice to call police but I took it from her.

"So you agree now?"

I have not change answer and said no.

"Let me call police from your flat. Police will see condition of my clothes and your semen on it. Next he will decide what to do."

I was scared and requested to stop such non sense. I was near door she pulled me in bedroom, pushed on floor and remove my night garment i.e. Lungee (a cloth bigger than towel in size wrapped around waist.) We both were nude.

"Let me enjoy my darling."

She climbed on me hold my dick in her hand and put it in her pussy. She was jumping up-down and enjoying.

"It is hard. She murmured—Eh eeh eeh oh aah aaah."

I was raped silently in a situation which neither I can accept nor reject.

"We must go in the bed for better sex enjoyment. Are you listening me or not?"

Silently we had gone to bed. She also came in bed from washroom. She enjoyed sex again. Since I was dragged in sex, so it was my turn to go up and put dick in her pussy and enjoy. She stayed with me whole the night because of heavy rain.

"What happened? Have you enjoyed?"

It was never happened in my life before. I have not had sex with stranger but with my wife only.

"You have not enjoyed? She asked me again."

No, you black mail me.

"Whatever you say, I enjoyed. You are handsome young and have strong cock and very good sex appeal. I really enjoyed and am happy. I got pleasure and relief."

It is 2 O'clock in night let us sleep.

"Forget time."

She holds and took my hand to her breast and asked me to rub it, most particularly nipples. I started rubbing slowly.

"Do it on both breasts with your both the hands."

I grabbed. I rubbed nicely and slowly pressed her breasts.

"Ah ah do like this please"

It is ok for you, you might have excited again.

"Yes, suck my nipples now one by one, climb on me enjoy hot sex and quench my thirst please."

I let her on bed faced up, sucked her nipples, enjoyed sex rubbing her breasts.

She was screaming and asking more, more and more. Later she asked a handy towel for cleaning her pussy."

I gave her very soft one and she cleaned.

"This is vaginal water. Do you know?"

No, I have enjoyed sex with my wife and she used to do these entire things.

"She cleaned her and your too like I did?"

Yes, I said.

"You know all the women are alike. Every woman produces this water just as lubricant to lubricate organs for good and full enjoyment."

I am not medico. You know about all these things better being medico. Let me sleep.

"No I want more. We have to enjoy whole the night and then we'll go for sleep."

She did foreplay to me and put my dick in her pussy and we both enjoyed this time vigorously. We sustain ejaculation longer than earlier. She was rubbing my back and shoulder while I was up on her. She felt light and tension free after sex.

"Kiss me? Kiss my nipples, I'll teach you how to enjoy the sex to its fullest."

I did whatever she wanted me to do.

"You again make me wet, let me clean it."

I ejaculated thrice but we manage sperm not to go inside her pussy.

"Can I get a glass of water and a cup of tea please?"

I gave her chocolate, water and later a cup of hot tea. I also took all with her.

"Once more we play before we go to sleep"

I laughed.

"Why you are laughing? She asked me"

I am trapped by you. You can enjoy with me as per your wish.

"That's like a good man, my man and only mine"

She finished tea and gone washroom to clean genital with water.

"Now I shall climb on you please lie down face up in the bed."

She switched on bedroom light and asked me to see what you have not seen in the dark."

She is slim and beautiful. Her skin is whitish in colour, curly black hair, big eyes, beautiful cheek, thin and long neck.

Her figure is 34-24-34. Her cup size is 34, round in shape with brown nipple. It was tight like virgin girl. I was really excited seeing her sexy curvaceous body!

It was her hairy pussy. She was up and enjoying pumping up and down on my dick.

"Don't see my face during this time. It will not be good. Once you she my face while having sex you'll not feel to have it again."

Really it was true. She looks very angry and her face was terrible. I am ejaculating now I told her. I hold her firmly from her shoulder and pushed dick fully in.

"No please no, just hold on few seconds more. Hold on please."

She was pushing harder and harder. We both ejaculated.

My genital area was full of white fluid as we both discharged out and she was sitting on it.

"I exhausted, completely exhausted."

She cleaned with towel. We both were exhausted.

"Let us enjoy this moment"

She asked me hold her while she was lying on my chest and giving me kisses. We both were nude and fell asleep holding each other. We don't know the time when we slept.

"Hi, it is ten thirty in the morning."

She gently touched and kissed me. How you will go home.

"I won't go home now."

What you will do.

"I'll fresh up and prepare breakfast for us, eat breakfast then decide what to do."

What you will wear? You had torn your dress.

"Don't worry I have another set of dress in my bag."

She gone in bathroom and I slept again.

She again wakes me up and dragged to washroom. I took shower and fresh up. We had toast butter and a glass of hot milk in the breakfast.

She told me on the breakfast table.

"I was craving and thirsty for three months. I decided to have sex with you. I saw you first at ticketing office, while you were collecting your air ticket. Agent told me madam don't worry this gentleman is also going with you. I had already collected mine. You asked him what time you should reach airport. Agent said 9.00 AM sharp you be there at airport."

"I was also told same timing by the agent. I decided to reach airport at the said time so that I can talk to you. I reached air port at quarter to nine and looking for you. I was upset because you have not reached till quarter to ten. Then at ten O'clock I saw you with agent. I wanted to talk to you but you disappeared. Where were you have been?"

I wanted a glass of water so agent took me to restaurant up stairs at the airport—Ashoka restaurant. I took water and juice. He paid for me and asked if I need anything else.

"Why you became late to reach airport?"

Agent send driver and called me in his office. He gave me some important letters and parcels for the fellow countrymen staying in this country. That's why I got delayed.

"I want to sit with you but you are late and I checked in with another lady and got seat with her."

[2]

"I WAS SCARED WHEN I SAW an old lady with you thinking she is your mother. That was reason why I could not talk to you in Singapore. When I saw you at Manila airport and the way you were helping others really I can't explain my feelings happiness and pleasure.

The help you extended to co-passengers in the Hotel was matchless. Without you we would have passed nights in transit lounge. I was so excited to see you when I came to you in the hotel for the help but you had not called me inside the room. I visited thrice but all the times you came out at the door and helped me and my sick friend."

I am not that type of man to allow stranger women in the room but as human being it is my duty to help you or any one if he or she needs my help.

"Today I make you. I win the game I planned?"

You blackmail me. You threaten me to do otherwise you will call police. I would have defamed and lost my job. This neither me nor my family would have tolerated. Now I'll be with you to fulfill your requirement.

"I promise to stick with you as your girl friend till the time we are here on the assignment. Once we back to native country, I pretend like we never met or never seen you."

Thanks for the idea otherwise our future life will become hell. People will hate us in our society. Our family life will ruin completely.

"I was really hungry for past few months. I feel extreme sexual sensation in me. I was very much excited when I hold you

---

12

in my arms and you ejaculated making my clothes wet. Even I don't care at that moment to take you in the bed."

I am also felt same thing. I was not prepared mentally but when you hold me I felt sexual sensations in me and can't stop myself.

"You are quite young and strong I felt it. Have you had sex with stranger earlier?"

No, I have never had sex with anyone other than my wife.

"You are my boy friend now. I am not a stranger to you. I'll tell my staff that you are not impotent. You are strong having good size of dick. Really! One can get pleasure having sex with you."

Why you will do that?

"It was one of my staff who came that night to you. She asked me if any young man came with me on assignment. She wanted to have sex with you. She is beautiful and slim like me but only drawback in her she drinks too much. Once she gets drunk needs a man who can satisfy her sexual desire. I told her your name and your house number. Rest already you know better."

I see, I wanted to hit her next time if have seen as my office staff told me that I might have seen ghost that night. No girl will do like that when I have narrated incident to them. Tell her not to come to me anymore.

"Sure now I am with you. I won't allow anyone to come near you."

She gave kiss to me again and again.

"I shall go to my flat, wash and iron my dress for tomorrow morning duty."

Well you please go now.

"What you are going to do?"

I am also going to wash all we have make dirty whole the night plus my clothes. I have to put all clothes in washing machine and wait to finish the wash.

I went in bathroom while she took duplicate key of main door of my flat from the key bunch.

"I can come to you any time my love."

No, before you come to me phone me, and then come. I do not want people say something bad about us.

"That's sounds better and intelligent step. My love you take care."

She left with duplicate key of my flat.

It was Sunday, I slept whole the day. I was thinking what happened was good or bad. At the end I came to conclusion that I couldn't stop myself. Her threat made me distress and fearful. I had no option but to go with her. If I had gone against her wish, I would have lost my job and reputation as well.

To save my Job and reputation I accepted her proposals unwillingly. I don't know if I had done right or wrong in your opinion but I did appropriate as per situation. I decided never allow her to enter my house again. What has happened is happened. Everything is over now. I slept peacefully. Four time sex with excited women in one night was not a joke. I sustained because I was young and craving for few months.

She called me at six in the evening.

"How are you my love? Did you sleep well? I also slept whole the day. I could not wash my clothes for morning duty. Did I disturb you?"

No not at all I replied her in formality. I am going for evening walk after evening tea.

"All right carry on then. We'll meet again."

No please do not do it again.

"Why what happened?"

Nothing happened forget it. What happened is happened.

"You go for evening walk please. I'll talk to you later when you come back from walk."

She disconnected phone without listening my reply.

I prepared tea and sipped slowly. I came out sky was clear no clouds. I took long walk. I walked approximately 7 km. It was 8 O'clock in the evening when I returned back. I prepared a glass of lime juice, switched on side lamps in dining hall, sit on sofa, and started enjoying my drink. I got scare with terrible sound heard inside my room. I came out looked here and there but could not see any one. I gone in side flat and switched all light ON even in bed room.

I removed my cloth for wash and gone for shower. I decided to take bath in the warm water in bath tub. I filled bath tub and entered in to the tub. Water was full I took dip in it and was relaxing.

I was scared when found someone putting hand on my head and rubbing. I cried out first.

"Don't worry my love this is me. I am at your service now. You should not take pain at all. Now on wards all your work is mine because you are mine."

First tell me how you entered in my flat? I had locked it and gone for evening walk. When and how you came in?

"You gone for walk then I took all my clothes and came to your flat and washed them. I know you will take at least one hour to return from the walk. I came in flat after you left for walk."

She entered in the tub sit on me holding my cock in hand. It got erected. We both had shower together.

"It is strong like iron rod. I love to have sex under shower"

She took cock inside her pussy. Since we were in tub she was finding it difficult to enjoy.

"Please stand up and switch shower on. I want to enjoy sex under shower."

We both stood under shower. I lift her little up to put cock in the pussy. She holds my body tightly with hand keeping her leg back on my thigh towards waist.

"It is hard like last night. Please push in side."

I pushed hard and she took support on small platform in washroom.

"Please push more! More!! Little more!!!"

I pushed as she desired and increased frequency pumping by taking little out.

"Yah yaa . . . h yee . . . h Oh she cried and loses her grip on me after ejaculation."

We both ejaculated. Shower was "on" she washed her and then mine too. I asked her to come out of the shower.

"Why?"

I have to prepare dinner.

"No, you need not to prepared dinner today."

Why? Then what we'll take?

"I have prepared dinner at my flat"

I can't go to your flat for dinner.

"I know that's why I have brought dinner in your flat."

I came out from washroom and performed evening prayer. She also finished shower and sit in prayer beside me.

"I shall prepare tea for you."

No, I have coffee for you. I purchased while coming back from work.

"You have coffee at home nice to know that. But I have developed taste of tea because you like tea."

I have coffee can you make two cups for both of us.

"Sure I shall."

She prepared two cups of coffee and brought in side bed room. She switched off main light and switch bed side lamps on.

"I like to sip coffee in pleasant atmosphere and in good mood. I created by switching bed side lamps "ON" since it is quite dim and switched off main light being bright."

I do not like coffee but to please her I said it is tasty. We finished coffee and chit—chat for quite some time. Now time is for dinner, let us go.

"Yes let me serve dinner."

She kept plates on dining table, warmed dinner and served it.

"How is dinner? Do you like my preparation?"

Yes dinner is delicious I like it. We finished dinner. I asked her to go in her flat.

"I hope you do not want me to repeat act which I did yesterday?"

No I am fully with you. I surrendered myself to you.

"All right let us go in the bed. I shall leave your flat early in the morning at six o'clock."

You must leave my flat by five in the morning.

"Why so early? She asked me"

Once you come out from your flat at six then you will know why I am asking you to leave flat by five o'clock."

"Tell me darling."

At six you will find two or three people on morning walk on the back side road and I am one of them.

"Thanks darling for this information. I shall leave you at five. Will you come with me?"

No, I'll be on the road till you reach your flat. I shall be visible till you reach your flat. Hope it is ok for you.

"Yes my love. It is too dark at 5 AM. Can I make it half pass five if o k"

Yes that's fine. I will come out first then give you indication that all are fine, you may leave.

"Darling now don't waste times let us go in the bed room."

You go and make bed ready I am coming. She was making bed, arranging bed sheet, pillows and taking blanket. I warmed two glasses of milk in microwave oven. I gave one to her and one for me.

"I had taken dinner in excess. Now you brought glass of milk. How I will take?"

No you have to take with me. She took one glass.

"For you I can take anything even poison too."

You have kids and women who love their kids never say anything bad.

"Have you finished your milk?"

No still some milk is in my glass.

"Can I see? Give me your glass?"

I gave my glass which she finished remaining milk in one sip.

"Let us enjoy this moment now."

She removed her cloth and just in panty and bra. She removed mine and makes me naked. She removed her panty and bra.

"You please come on me and enjoy but be careful do not ejaculate inside. I am very sensitive even a drop is sufficient for me to get pregnant."

I shall try my best to take all precautions not to make you pregnant.

"Well come on now."

She holds my cock in the hand. It was already erected. She set it properly in her pussy.

"Now you push in side. Push little more."

I pushed in hard she cried in pleasure. She gripped my back by both hands and started rubbing my back. I was enjoying sex pushing as much as she wanted and increased frequency as per her desire.

"Let me clean I am wet she asked me."

While I was taking cock out I ejaculate out on her pussy.

"You also ejaculated."

Yes I am. She cleaned her first then mine. While she was cleaning again erection took place. We went back in the bed.

"It is still hard. We can enjoy still more. It is my turn to go up."

She climbed up, took cock in her pussy and asked me to rub her breast. I rubbed her breasts and she got excited.

"Please suck my nipples."

She holds me on my back while I was sucking her nipples. She increased her frequency pumping fast, crying and working on the tip of cock then pushed whole cock inside her pussy while crying—eeah! eeah!!, in the pleasure.

"Ah I am wet again and exhausted. Let me clean. You ejaculated again?"

Yes darling. I replied.

"You dropped inside my pussy?"

No. I replied. When you took out my cock from your pussy I ejaculated.

"Then fine."

But you have to take precautionary action.

"What precautionary action you mean?"

Go in wash room clean with water. Even you can take water through pipe little pushing inside your vagina. It will clean all from inside. You apply little perfume it will be fine.

"My love can you help me. I am still feelings to have sex?"

Yes, I am too. You clean first with water. I helped her cleaning and perfuming her pussy.

I cleaned mine and spray perfume on it.

"Why you have perfumed our sex organ?"

I did it by chance if ejaculation takes place inside, you should be safe from getting pregnant.

"It is good idea. Now you may start. Do you know some best poses? If yes then let us enjoy sex in different poses. I won't mind giving you pose."

Today we'll enjoy normal sex. Next week we enjoy in different poses.

"Who will wait for next week? I'll come whenever I want. Nobody can stop me. I am having duplicate key of this house."

No, before you come to me always call me first darling. If someone with me I'll tell you not to do so.

"O.K.I trusts you. Now let us enjoy."

She kissed me and I kissed her too. We enjoyed sex this time little longer. She was happy and enjoyed more as duration was longer. I ejaculated finally.

"I am tired now but feeling quite relaxed."

She cleaned genital area with soft towel and dropped it on floor. I hold her breasts and pressed gently. Warm breath experienced on each other faces. I kissed her at neck, cheek and her lips. After some time, we slept holding each other.

Alarm was buzzing. It was set for five in the morning.

"Let me go washroom first. I shall give you morning kiss before I go."

She kissed me before going washroom. I went in kitchen to make tea and coffee for me and her.

"Can you please come inside wash room?"

What happened?

"I want to brush my teeth but I have no brush. Do you have spare brush?"

I'll give you a temporary for time being. Later I buy for you a good brush. I gave her one tooth brush which was supplied by air hostage in air craft. I asked her to manage with this.

"So nice of you providing me brush darling. Thank you so much"

I said welcome to her and left for kitchen. Tea was boiling I added milk to it and slow down stove.

She called me again.

"I am using your towel hope you won't mind."

Darling when you make me yours then here everything is yours. Be quick your coffee is ready. I told her while I was brushing my teeth.

"So you make coffee for me."

Of course yes, I have to keep your choice first.

I boiled milk and prepared a cup of coffee. She was ready by that time. We both took tea and coffee in the morning. Hurry up it is half past five.

"OK darling."

She kissed me and touched my cock. I kissed her too.

"Bye darling see you later. Come let us go now."

I came out first and checked all around no one was on the road. Road was clear. I hinted her to come out as nobody was on road. She came out and gone to her flat. She gave me flying kiss when reached her flat.

I started washing machine as load of dirty clothes were kept in it then gone to washroom.

Telephone was ringing. I took it and said—hello.

"Hi it's me darling."

You reached your flat. Did anyone saw you?

"No, no one met me."

That's good. Tell me why you have called me?

"I left my under garment in your washroom. Can you please hide them somewhere? I don't want anyone see these in your room."

O. K. I shall take care, anything else?

"No, Nothing. My sweet kisses to my love."

I got sweet kisses.

"Bye bye"

Bye.

I put bed sheet, towel, under garments, in washing machine, washed and hanged them on rope. I took shower, performed prayer and took my breakfast. I locked door and went out to get transport to go to office. My co-worker has office vehicle picked me. I reached office in ten minutes and resumed my duties.

I was busy at work as being first day of the week. Lots of complains were there from clients. One by one we fixed problems and back to office at quarter to twelve.

Lunch time starts from twelve till half pass one. I reached home at quarter pass twelve. I took out left over of evening from fridge and kept on the table. I changed my dress, baked few chapattis. I warmed left over soup and vegetables in microwave.

I was at dining table eating my lunch while telephone rang. I brought telephone near table, lifted and said hello.

"This is me my love. How are you?"

I am fine eating my lunch. Have you taken your lunch?

"I am sorry, I disturbed you. I'll call you later."

She disconnected line.

I finished lunch gone in the bed to take rest. Telephone rang again. I lifted phone and wanted to say hi darling but I heard male voice on other side.

He asked—"Have you finished your lunch?"

I replied—Yes. Then I asked who is there?

—I am from air port control room. There is some problem in the machine at airport. Can you please come and check it. A flight is expected in 30 minutes time.

I'll be there in 15 minutes—I replied.

Ok that will be fine—airport staff replied.

I called my colleague and informed him the problem at airport machine. He said—"I am coming to pick you. You should get ready."

I was getting ready while telephone buzzed again. Lifted phone and heard-

"Hi darling why you kept you telephone busy?"

I got a call from airport staff and then I called my staff to take me to airport. I am getting ready for air port to attend problem. I'll call you from office.

"No, I am calling from other number not from my office. I'll call you in the office."

No you should not call me in the office. What time you will finish your duty?

"Three o'clock in the afternoon. I'll be at home by 3.30 pm."

Then I shall call you when I get time after 3.30 pm.

"On your home or mine number."

You must be available at your home number.

"Fine then I'll be at my home."

I'll call you, once I get time.

"I'll wait for your call."

I could not get time at work to call her. I thought I give call from my home. It would be safe and good to talk from home rather than office.

I finished my duties and back to home at five in the evening. As usual I prepared my tea and took some biscuits, sit at table and enjoyed. I took little rest on sofa kept in the dining hall. I phoned her.

"Hi darling"

How you know it is me?

"You told me that you will call me. So I was waiting for your call."

You must confirm who other side is before saying darling otherwise someone else will come in our way.

"Sorry darling, I'll obey you. Forgive me this time. I was eagerly waiting for your call. Telephone buzzed then I could not stop, lifted phone and said darling. You are right I must confirm who other side is?"

It is fine. We must take precaution on phone calls.

"What is your plan?"

I am going for evening walk. My time and works are fixed. You can say time table is fixed.

"Fine then you carry on."

I got ready for evening walk at six. I met one of the friends on the way. He was also on evening walk. We both back at my home after walk. It was half past seven.

I prepared two glasses of lemon water and we were sipping lemon juice when telephone buzzed. I knew who is calling. I took telephone said hello! Who is there disturbing my rest. I just back from evening walk.

"Hi darling it is me, your love. Who is there with you?"

I told the name of the friend.

"I hope you are telling truth."
No, not at all give me some time I'll call you when I get ready.
"That's fine darling but get ready quick."
My friend asked me who was on other side.
I told him-Call was from office, emergency call.

'Then I must leave you quick. I wanted to pass this evening with you. We have not sat together since quite long—my friend said.'

Yes, it is true. I'll take shower and then go. You can sit 10 to 15 minutes more.

'No, now I'll leave you—my friend said.' Further he said he going to market with a local guy working with him in his section. He may be coming now to pick me.

He left my home. I closed my door and locked from inside. I phoned her. It was ringing I was murmuring lift the phone darling. Then I got reply. "Hello!" Seems other side is a sick lady. Her voice was vibrating. I disconnected telephone immediately. Who is this lady? What she is doing in her flat? I'll get all information from Sandra, my love, once I get her call.

I rushed in bathroom for fresh up. I took shower, finished prayer and prepared tea. I was eagerly waiting her call. I was walking in the dining room from one side to other.

Telephone ranged I became happy. I lifted phone. This call was from office, real emergency call. I was picked up by my friend and gone to attend fault. I called her from there. No response from her. Now I was upset. Where she might have gone at this time?

I came back home and open door. It seems someone running towards my bed room. I said sit down John. I am coming. I rush to bedroom, switched light on; I could not find any one. Since no one was with me, I phoned again to my love. No one was lifting phone. I shouted where she might have gone!

When she knew I am alone. She came out of mini storeroom.

"I am here darling do not shout. I am coming in your arms in a minute."

She came quickly and sat in my lap. She tempted me. I kissed her. She kissed me too. I hold her tightly and kissed her cheek and took her lips in mouth and started chewing.

"I'll die in your arms."

Don't say such word again.

"You love me so much?"

Yes, you made me like this. I was something else. I was far—far away from these things. I did not know what is love?

"You know I am very happy with you. I want to pass rest of my life under your arms."

It is nine in night. Let us prepare some dinner.

"I was cutting vegetable when I heard sound of your car I rushed to bedroom. When you said—sit down John. I got scared and hide myself in storeroom. I hold my breath when you entered in bedroom and switched lights on. When you phoned and murmuring—where she might have gone? Why she is not lifting phone? I knew you are alone and could not stop myself and fell in your arms. When you hold me tight in your arms I felt sensation and asked you to kiss me. I know you love me so much."

We derived a code for telephone call. Either of us wants to contact other will ring once and hang the telephone. This will indicate us from where call was. Then second time phone rings immediately follow this can be taken and answered as per situation. Don't say darling etc if someone with you. This is because the guest with you may not able to know who was on line from other side.

"This is good idea. It is fine we must practice."

Let us start cooking dinner. You be at stove and do cooking. I'll help you.

"I am ready darling."

She started cooking vegetable. I washed lentil and kept in pressure cooker on second stove. I asked her if she will take rice or managed with breads.

"Breads will be fine. I had enough rice in lunch."

I kneaded flour, made breads (Chapattis). Mean while lentil soup was ready so I fried it. Now dinner was ready. I asked her to come on table.

"Let me wash my hands and face."

I kept plates and brought all the food on the table. I asked her to join me.

"I am here on the table. What should I do?"

Take one plate and I started serving food. She took plate, served, pray God and started eating dinner.

I asked her. Who answered my phone at your place in the evening?

"She was an elderly lady. I don't know her name. She came for medicine. She told me that line got disconnected. Who was other side I have asked her."

One should not lift the telephone if he or she in other's house. This is not a good habit. Some time it develops confusion and even causes separation in the family.

"Of course yes, you are right while I was coming to take the phone she lifted and was talking. I asked her who other side was. She replied line got disconnected."

We finished dinner. She also joined me with her glass of milk. She developed habit taking milk after dinner like me. We were in bedroom and enjoying warm milk.

"Today we'll enjoy different poses. You tell me which pose you like."

I lie down in the bed and asked her to sit on my cock facing towards my feat. She did that.

"What is next—she asked me"

Take cock inside and enjoy. I sat on the bed and rubbing her breast. She can see herself in the mirror of dressing table which was kept in bedroom at leg side.

"I am not getting enough space to move up and down on the dick. I am in fixed position. You hold my breast and pushed cock fully in. How can I enjoy?"

I lie down again leaving her breast and asked if she is comfortable now.

"Yah. eeh! Let me enjoy. You be in the same position. Please do not get up. If you get up I'll not able to enjoy. Please do not talk to me for a moment."

Ok I will not change my position. She was pumping up down very fast. Aah Aah aaah! She cried while pumping fast.

"I am wet darling hold me in your arms."

I hold her in my arms and told her that I also ejaculated. "What, you have ejaculated in me? She cried."

No it won't go inside because you are sitting. My genital area is full of discharge of us. She got up quickly and gone in washroom to clean it. She saw my genital area was full of fluid.

"Let me clean mine first then I shall clean your later. Just wait please."

I gone in washroom and she cleaned with water. She back in bed and after one hour she again enjoyed same pose.

"It is giving more pleasure to me. I can see in the mirror cock is going fully in pussy. I can take cock fully in—in this way."

But I am ejaculating quickly in this pose. Please enjoy in medium pace and clean your genital frequently.

"You should try to stop it. If you tell me I'll stop at that moment and after few seconds you may be as good as earlier. I'll clean and then start again"

She back in action after cleaning with soft towel. May I rub your breasts?

"That is not possible in this pose. You can do that later. Let me enjoy this pose."

She increased frequency and I asked her to be slow. She thought I ejaculated. She took my cock out cleaned and again took inside her pussy.

She sat on her feet keeping side by my waist took cock in and started pumping. I feel more pleasure but ejaculated soon.

"You ejaculated inside? I do not want to carry baby."

I don't want you to get pregnant otherwise we both will be in trouble.

"Let me clean. I shall try this pose one more time today. I am enjoying."

She cleaned my cock while she wanted to take inside her pussy I stopped her and took one rubber band put around the cock. Then I asked her to enjoy now.

"She took my cock in and then started fucking. She was murmuring and telling me it is strong and getting thick. Why you have not put rubber band first?"

I asked her that it is my turn now let me fuck.

"No, I am still enjoying—she was crying in joy—Ah Aah Aaah Yah ouch I exhausted."

I asked her to go clean with water.

"I am tired in this pose. Let me take rest for few minutes then I shall go and clean."

Ok. You take rest I am going washroom.

"Please clean yourself. I am not in position to clean you right now. I can but you have to wait few minutes."

I hold her in my arms and took her in washroom.

"Let me clean your first and then I clean mine"

She cleaned mine and later her. She kissed my cock. What are you doing? I asked her.

"I am kissing."

You are kissing cock? It is dirty thing. I am getting hot.

"I was craving for this. You are telling me it is dirty thing. For me it is good thing."

I gave some sweet to her and took some. We took glass of water.

"Hey I am fresh again. Very fresh! Is this effect of sweet?"

Yes, sweet gives instant energy when you are tired. Now it is my turn, don't say you will enjoy again.

"Ok this is your turn now. You tell me how you want to have sex."

She lay down face up. I kept her both the legs on my shoulder. She took my dick inside her pussy. I lean towards her chest and gently rubbed her breasts while pushing hard inside her pussy.

"No, No, it is hard and painful please take out. I shall set it properly."

I took out she set it and asked me to push. I pushed and gently rubbed her breasts while pumping slowly in the same pose. She was crying and getting pleasure also. I am sorry my love. I could not stop as I was getting more pleasure.

"It was little painful but was full of enjoyment. We do this pose tomorrow again."

Just think of today forget tomorrow. Nobody has seen tomorrow.

"Why do you say that nobody has seen tomorrow?"

Because tomorrow turns into today!!!

We both laughed and laughed longer.

"Today you make me happy not only with my sexual desire but you cut good jokes too."

It was quite late in night. We took some ice cream then I asked her to sleep now.

"Please hold me in your arms and we'll sleep"

We hold each other in arms; her breast was touching my chest. I was feeling good. I kissed her and said good night.

"Good night you too"

We get relaxed and slept till alarm buzzed at 5 AM. I asked her to get up and be ready to go.

"Why morning came so soon? God should have night longer than day."

Please get up and get ready to leave my flat before anyone see you going from here.

"I shall sleep here today. I have night duty. You get ready and go to work. I'll prepare lunch for you and meet at lunch."

No, you should go early home my love otherwise someone may see you cooking lunch at my place then it will be problem for us.

"Nobody will see me. Sleep, still there is time for your morning walk darling."

I slept holding her in my arms. Her breast was against my chest. I tighten my grip.

"My darling you don't make me crazy early in the morning."

What about morning session my love?

"You want morning session then come on we shall have morning session too."

We had sex early in the morning. It was great pleasure each time we had sex. After sex we both slept again. It was 8 in the morning when we got up. I was quite late for work. I should be at work by this time.

"Take morning session—she taunted and laughed—ha ha ha!"

I am late you are laughing!!!

"You go for bath. I shall make breakfast and tea for you in the mean time."

Let me call my office then I will act accordingly.

"I am going to prepare your breakfast whatever you think you do."

I rang office and requested some to come and pick me up.

My colleague told me to attend a fault at airline main office which was near my home. Mean while he is sending messenger to pick me from that office. I should call him after fixing the fault.

I agreed. I took shower and asked her to take shower also. We both had shower and finished prayer. Later we took breakfast. It was 8:45 AM. I kissed her and left for Airline main office to attend the fault.

I attended air line ticketing system and fixed problem quick. I called my office to pick me up after completion of the work. Messenger came to pick me. He asked me to drop him at his residence, take car and go to office.

I dropped him at his residence and started for office. It was ten when I reached office.

There was not much work in the office but I could not contact her. Office staff noticed some changes in me.

You look very happy today—one of the staff asked me.

Same girl, who came to his flat nude, might have visited him again—other staff taunted.

No, I am happy because I got letter from home and all is fine over there. I lied to them.

May I join you at dinner in your flat?—A lady staff asked me.

You are welcome at lunch. Why you are asking for dinner? I replied.

No, lunch break is too short. I do not want lunch. I want to spend more time with you and that is possible at dinner only. She further explained me that best time for dinner with me is Friday and she want to stay till Monday morning with me. Then we both together come to office on Monday morning.

Sorry, I do not have that much time. I can't spare—I said.

It was 12 noon so I left for lunch. I reached at flat and open door.

"Lunch is ready darling, she told me while she took off my shirt."

Let me wash my hand mean while you arrange plates.

"I am going to serve lunch in plates on dining table"

No, bring lunch in the bedroom. We use tea table to take lunch.

She brought lunch in the bedroom and kept on tea table lying there.

"Start lunch now."

We started lunch. Lunch is very nice. I passed my complement. It is really finger liking.

"Thanks at least someone appreciated my preparation. I was never got appreciation for food preparation by my husband. He is better cook than me. He always pointed on weak points. Chilly is too much, Salt is too much, some time he commented oil is not used etc but never appreciated that food is nice. This is first time someone appreciated and liked my cooking."

It is really tasty lunch. I repeated again.

"Shall I give some more?"

No, I am full now. I can't eat any more. I am going to take little rest. I gone in the bed and soon fell asleep. She cleaned plate and tea table, arranged left over in the fridge. She also came in the bed and kissed me. I requested no sex at this time otherwise I might not able to go office.

"Darling it is ok. I am just kissing you and holding you in my arms. It gives me pleasure. Shall I continue?"

It is ok you may continue like this. We took a snap. She got up at quarter pass one in afternoon. She prepared a cup of tea for me and coffee for her.

"Your tea is ready. Please fresh up, have your tea and get ready for office."

I thanked her.

"Why you always say thanks when I do some work?"

I am habitual to thank people who help me in any way. So it is appreciation for you.

"Don't be late in the evening."

I shall try to come early.

"Let me kiss again"

We kissed each other. I reached office on time. There was no complaint from clients. I was busy in office work. Suddenly I saw, it was five in evening. I started for home and reached within fifteen minutes.

"I was waiting for you."

What happened?

"Nothing, I love you most. You are my real love, actually real love that's why"

I asked her a cup of coffee.

"Sure, I shall prepare coffee. Take some biscuit first and then coffee."

All right, I wash my hand and fresh up then we both had some biscuits and a cup of coffee.

"I was in my flat during afternoon."

How you have gone? Did someone see you going out from my flat?

"I came out no one was there so I gone to my flat. I had just arrived ten minutes before you."

You should not take risk like this. During day from these houses, being glass doors, everyone can see who is on the road from inside but person on the road can't see in side. You can see who is sitting inside the hall but they can't see anyone who is there on the road during night time. It is just opposite that of day time. Next time do not do this.

"Thanks you have informed me. Darling, I was not aware of this. I saw no one was on the road so I gone to my flat. I am sorry. I shall always obey you."

That' likes my true love. Now I shall go for evening walk. What you are going to do?

"I shall go to my flat to pick dinner already prepared. I'll bring when you call me after you back from evening walk. I shall iron my dress. I am on night duty and will leave you at 10 pm."

Ok then I'll leave you. I am going for the evening walk.

"I don't want live alone. Can't you stop your evening walk today?"

Right, I shall not go for evening walk today. What should do I do now?

"You want to have sex right now."

No. Why? Only sex is there in the life? There is nothing else which we can share.

"Hey, rain started. Credit comes to me. I stopped you from going for evening walk otherwise you were wet in the rain."

Let us make some hot stuff right now.

"Like what?"

Like chilly or bread pakoras.

"What you need to make pakoras?"

You don't know what ingredients required for pakoras?

"No, really don't know. When we need we get it from market."

I'll teach you what is required for and how pakoras are prepared. Clean two onions, chopped it thin and long.

"Please tell me step by step so that next time I may prepare for you."

She pealed onion and chopped as desired. She learned now chopping onion for pakoras.

I gave chickpeas flour two—three table spoon and asked her to add a pinch of salt and chilly power.

"Just see how much I have to add salt and chili powder."

Quarter tea spoon salt and one spoon chilli power is fine.

"Ok now what is next? Shall I add water or onion?"

You add first onion and then little water and mixed it till become semisolid. She did it. I asked to put frying pan on stove, add cooking oil in it and heat. She did that.

"Oil is hot now"

I took small portion of mixture and dropped in the hot oil slowly. I asked her to do like I have done. She also put mixture like I did and made pakoras.

"When I have to take pakoras out of frying pan?"

Just fry it till become golden brown.

"See! It is golden brown now."

Take all out of frying pan.

"Leave the kitchen. I'll fry all. Now I know how to prepare."

She prepared all and then kept water on stove for making tea. We both enjoyed pakoras.

"It is nice and hot."

It will make you hot too.

"What do you mean?"

I shall tell you after tea. She brought tea and we both took tea.

"Tell me now?"

I took her in the bed and put blanket on her as Air condition was on.

"Please come in the blanket."

I was inside blanket. She took my cock in her hand.

"Hey it is tight and hard like steel rod."

Now you know I told you pakoras make you hot.

"Let us have sex."

I said ok. We enjoyed sex in the evening itself. It was very vigorous. We got much pleasure. This was second round in the day. We generally do two to three rounds in a day. We enjoyed sex.

"I am tension free and feeling very light now. Thanks for all these and satisfying my sexual desire. Now I shall go for duty. You sleep now no one will disturb you."

We took some rest. She requested to come in her flat for dinner. We both gone to her flat, had dinner followed by ice cream.

"Kiss me and go now. Staff van may come to pick me any moment."

I kissed her and left for my flat. I reached in my flat. She practiced phone calling code which we mutually set.

She rang once and hanged then again rang till I lift receiver. I know this is her call. I lifted and answered hi honey how are you?

"My darling code is working wonderful. I was testing it, Bye for now?"

Bye bye.

We enjoyed the sex more often. She was much pleased and happy.

Past three months we had no sex. So enjoyment was very—much exciting. We had felt relaxed after having sex. One day we did one pose likewise we had done many.

We had sex on sofa, under shower, in bathtub, standing poses, dog pose, on the table, swinging pose against pillar just few to name them.

[3]

ONE EVENING I WAS SITTING quiet. She felt that I am thinking something as I was not talking to her.

"Are you feeling you have done wrong?"

I replied yes I am thinking and feeling also.

"She asked me why?"

I must have sexual relation with my wife only not with other women.

"What I have seen in the movies I will make it true."

She went in prayer room and called me there. She took pot of vermilion. She took a pinch of vermilion, kept it on my hand and then put my hand on her forehead. The vermilion was applied on her head.

"Now I am your wife. We are husband and wife in front of God. I am declaring that I am your wife. What we have done earlier was correct not sin. You satisfied me in all respect, you love me. God will help you always."

Darling it is fine, works in films only. I am ok.

"I beg you from God. You might have not noticed it. I always sit in prayer with you as husband and wife."

No, I have not noticed it. I always pray God closing my eyes and concentrating on Him. I am not looking at that time here and there. When I sit for prayer who is doing what I do not know. I concentrate in meditation during that period.

"Now you must not repent my darling. Do you agree?"

Yes I agree, I said to her. I do not want any arguments.

"I am going night duty"

Ok. I kissed her.

It was Friday. I watched movie late in night at my friend's house. I return my flat at 3 AM and slept.

It was eight in the morning I was in sound sleep. She came from duty in my flat and open door quietly. She entered in the bedroom and came in the bed. She kissed and wake mc up.

"I want to entertain you in a special pose in my uniform. This will be special pose from me to my love."

She was lean down on knee and elbow in the bed and asked me to strip and hold her waist and push cock in her pussy.

We enjoyed sex in this pose though see was cried little but feel nice. This was dog pose.

"I shall hold you in my arms and sleep. What happen today you are sleeping at this time?"

I watched movie at friend's house and came late. It was three in the morning when I return home.

We got up at half past nine. She cooked breakfast while I was in washroom.

"Let us have bubble bath today. I'll fill tub with lukewarm water and you squeeze bubble soap. Let us be in the tub together."

We entered in the tub and she rubbed my back while I rubbed her.

"You lie in the tub. I want to have sex in the tub."

She sat on my thigh holding my dick in hand, positioned to her pussy and then pushed in. It slipped in smoothly due to soapy water.

She was enjoying sex in the tub. We were on apex of the sex and ejaculated inside her pussy.

"Don't worry it is fine. I am in the period. During period if you drop semen inside me will not get pregnant."

You know all these better. I am scared that sex should not be cause of defame. We can't survive with bad name.

"I know and will take utmost care of that. I am thankful to you from deep my heart for all the help and satisfying me.

Menstruation period is of one week from the date of start. Generally five to six days bleeding took place and then it is clear. Just after this till 10 days are very crucial and ejaculation in side may lead to pregnancy. After this ten days till next ten days very safe for sex no fear of the pregnancy. This is safe period to enjoy. Ten days before the menstruation period dangerous zone. If ejaculation takes place inside then pregnancy is sure."

I learn a good thing from her about menstruation cycle and pregnancy time zone. I was not aware earlier about this.

"Look water in the bath tub. It is red because of my bleeding. Please drain the water and have shower now."

I drain the water and open shower. She was behind me rubbing my back.

"Give me soap I'll apply on you."

She applied soap on me and I applied on her. We both had shower. We took little coconut oil in the palm and put some water then applied on each other's body to keep soft whole the day. We went for prayer and after prayer we took breakfast.

"I am tired now want to sleep. Will you go to market?"

What do you need from market?

"Today green vegetables available from local farm in the market one of my staff told me."

I shall go then. I love green vegetables. Do you need anything else?

"No, I do not want anything."

I dressed, got ready started car and reached market. I picked up green vegetables, tomatoes, peas, beer and ice cream. I went office to check system status and then back to home.

She was in sound sleep. I cooked lunch—green vegetable, soup, rice and bread.

I woke her up at half pass one in afternoon. Darling fresh up lunch is ready. Here is a can of beer for you.

"Let me sleep. I don't feel hungry."

You eat lunch and then sleep again. She got up from the bed and called me.

"Look your bed sheet is dirty."

I asked her what happened.

"I got menstruation today and bleed out. My bleeding spoils your bed sheet."

Don't worry. Put bed sheet for wash in the washing machine add soap, bleaching agent and start. Machine will clean everything.

"I shall wash this before go for lunch."

Washing machine is automatic. Put clothes, soap, cleaning agent and start. It will do all and give you clean clothes.

"All right then I'll put clothes, soap and bleaching agent and start the machine."

She got fresh up after putting clothes for laundry. She sits on the table and sipping beer.

"My tension is released today."

What tension you had?

"I did not receive my period on time. It was fear in me that I might have got pregnant. Numbers of time you fell off semen inside me. I was doubtful that your sperm might have gone in ovary and I got pregnant."

Thanks God everything is fine. You take very vigorous sex with me every time. Take care to avoid pregnancy.

"I am happy today. Can I get one more beer please?"

Yes why not. It is in the fridge. I shall give you wait a moment.

"No, I will help myself. I have to remove laundry and hang clothes for dry. Now machine is stopped."

She removed laundry and hanged for drying. She took a can of beer and came on table.

"Bring lunch on dining table now."

Spinach in vegetable, soup, chapatti and rice I brought on the table. Plates were lying on the table since beginning.

"You start please—she said to me."

I took my plate and she took her. I served lunch in the plates. We said grace and started lunch.

"Lunch is tasty It is finger licking."

I brought roasted papad and gave her.

"It is good and goes well along with beer."

Do you need more?

"Give me one more."

I gave one more papad to her. We enjoyed lunch with taste and finished.

I asked her ice cream.

"No, we shall take ice cream later. I don't want to spoil taste of lunch."

As you wish.

"Where is other bed sheet? I shall make your bed."

It is in the chest drawer in the bedroom. She took a bed sheet, arranged bed, kept pillows and blanket.

"Bed is ready come let us take rest."

Have you taken napkin? If not please take otherwise this bed sheet will also be spoiled.

"Yes, I have taken Napkin."

We slept till half past five in the evening.

"Let me go bathroom. Then I shall make tea for you. Please wait."

I was still in the bed. She used bath room and later prepared tea for us.

"Tea is ready—she called me."

I sipped tea and gone for evening walk. She did ironing of the clothes—her dress, my shirt, paints, bed sheets etc. After that she left for her flat.

I back from evening walk took lime water, taken rest and then gone for shower.

I was in prayer when she back in my flat again.

"I have cooked dinner, brought it and kept on the cooking range."

May I get a cup of tea?—I asked her.

"Will you take tea now?"

Yes please.

"I think take a can of beer it would be nice."

Do not take much in the evening. We had already taken two cans in the lunch.

Let us take coffee and we'll take beer at half pass nine. Dinner may be served at ten or half pass ten. What do you say?

"I shall make coffee."

She prepared two cups of coffee and gave one to me.

"Here is your cup of coffee."

We enjoyed hot coffee. I switched on radio and enjoyed music.

I was Radio Jokey during those days and giving the weekly radio programme for one hour in my native language. We took dinner and then gone in bed. We both have to go for work in the morning. We slept till alarm buzzed.

[4]

PURCHASED A CAR FOR MY personal use. We generally go for outing after dinner in the car and enjoying cool fresh breeze. Then we go to bed.

It was my turn to go her flat and enjoy sex with her. She was beautiful tall and slim. I am feeling her warm breath. It is still touching my heart. I am feeling she is with me even now. Though her flat was little away but she manages to come to my flat.

"I was coming to your house people watching me. Some of them even asked me where I am going."

Forget it tell them my name say I am going to see him. Let them come and ask why she is coming to you.

"Don't be angry honey. I am telling you curiosity of the peoples."

One Sunday she came from duty at half pass three in after noon. She entered in my flat. She had lunch and then had sex with me. She kept all her cloth on the chair kept near bed in bedroom. Chair was visible from hall. She forgot to close main door. We were holding each other enjoying moment after sex. One of my friends knocked my back door which is on main road side. I did not respond to his call. I was busy with my love enjoying kisses. Once she is in my house I do not allow anyone to come in.

My friend came to main door and entered in the hall because door was left open. He called me shouting my name. My love jumped from bed and took her clothes and hide in the mini store room which is attached to bedroom.

I came out and pretend that I was sleeping. He asked me why I left my door open.

I replied—I am suffering from allergy so I open door and rushed for medicine. I got a call from home while taking medicine. I was on phone and forgotten to close door. I slept after talking on phone and still feel sleepy because effect of medicine.

He wanted to accompany me in evening walk after taking tea at my house. I acted well and asked him if he will take tea.

You sleep now I am going for walk will take tea some time later.

He left my house. I closed door from inside.

Darling what you did? I asked her.

"I am sorry love. I was so excited for sex that I forgotten to close the door."

You left door open and my friend came in the hall. What would have been our position if he had entered in the bedroom?

"I am really sorry. He would have exposed us in the community if he has seen both of us in bed and naked."

Be careful for next time. Do not leave door open darling. You must double check the door if it is closed properly.

"Sure I was stupid gone mad for you and forgotten to close door."

Our love was going on. We were enjoying life at full swing. Every day we were experimenting sex at new height. One day I asked her I want your pussy hairless. Hair around your genital area is long enough. Why can't you remove it?

"You have hair similar to mine on your genital. I also want cock without hair."

We both laughed on this. What a topic of discussion. We were silent for few moments after this. You shave mine and later I'll shave yours.

"I think today is not right time. I'll bring disposable razors then do shaving.

Where from you are bringing razors?

"I'll bring from the Hospital. There are plenty razors and used in operations."

Well I am having mine in the bathroom.

"You are using that for shaving beard. Don't spoil that. You can't wait a day?"

All right let it be next day. I am tired today.

"I shall give you massage where you have kept oil."

It is in bathroom in the drawer. She open drawer and asked me.

"There are two bottles which one I'll bring."

Bring coconut oil bottle.

"You like massage with coconut oil."

I like your soft touch with oil.

"Remove your clothes."

I removed all clothes except underwear. She stripped off that too. I was nude lying on the bed.

"I am coming let me removed mine."

She was also nude. She gave massage to me. She applied oil on my body and gave a gentle touch with her hand. She asked me to be upside down and gave massage on my back.

She rubbed my back with her breast. I felt pleasure.

"Today is Sunday, your holiday. You are tired by sleeping. I have done my duty. It was too tiresome. Numbers of accidents cases were there. I am tired too."

You lie down on the bed. I shall give massage to you.

"No. I do not want that my love take pain for me."

I hold her and pulled in the bed. She was in my lap.

"First let us have sex then give me massage."

I shall give massage then have sex.

"No then I shall get sleep while you give massage to me."

I won't allow you to sleep.

"Then all right go ahead and give massage."

I gave her massage on whole body. When I notice she fell sleepy I rub her breast. Breast was round and was slipping because on oil. She murmured in pleasure.

"Leave me a moment please. I am going in bathroom."

She back from bathroom applied oil on my cock and started foreplay.

I asked her not to do this otherwise I'll ejaculate outside soon.

"Wait let me climb on. Which postures you want enjoy sex today?"

I am lying down face up on the bed. You sit on my cock facing toward my face and stretch both the legs towards my shoulder. You then try to hold my shoulder with your hand and start enjoying.

"I am doing that if it is not proper please correct me."

You are sitting right. You hold my shoulder and enjoy now. She was pumping fast. Because of oil it was so smooth and soft. She was enjoying.

"Ah aah! It is lovely. It has gone fully in. It is hard like rod. It is giving me more pleasure. Oil is adding smoothness in the sex and more enjoyment."

She started slowly then speeded up. I asked her—let me enjoy also.

"No me first. Do not ejaculate please. Keep it tight. I will take few seconds more."

I put my thumb on her genital and rubbed it.

"Yeeh ah aah! What are you doing? I aroused now. Please stop rubbing my clitoris."

She ejaculated and exhausted. She fell in my arms. I also ejaculated and hold her firmly in my arms. We were in this pose for few minutes. Later she cleaned our genital area which was full of sperm. We both slept holding each other under blanket.

We got up at six in the evening. We took bath, then a cup of tea and little snacks.

"I am going to my flat to bring something for dinner."

Why? I am having plenty things in the fridge for dinner. You can cook whatever you like.

"OK, are you going for walk?"

No I have taken shower today. I shall not go for walk. I shall be with you and enjoy time with you.

"We had enough enjoyment today after dinner we shall sleep."

Darling as you wish.

"Can you bring some beer for drink? We shall enjoy drink today."

I am going to bring beer. Lock the door from inside. Do not open even any one knock the door.

"Nobody will do that. If your car is not there then who will knock the door?"

I managed to get four cans of beer from hotel bar. I came back to my house. I open the door. I gave her cans of beer.

"I have prepared Pakoras when you gone to bring beer. It goes well with beer."

She sits on sofa nearby me. In one plate she brought pakoras. She open cans of beer and poured in glasses.

"This is your glass. She gave me one and said cheers!"

Cheers for my love!!! Slowly we sipped two cans of beers. We feel little drowsy.

"What is time now?"

It is only nine in the evening.

"Do you have more beer?"

No, but I can bring if you need more.

"No, I am fine with two cans of beer. Let us go for dinner."

We wash hand and face to become fresh and came on dining table. I asked her—if she has cooked something for dinner.

"Yes I cooked your favourite dish. You guess."

Tell me please. I can't guess which one as I have list of favourite dishes.

"Paratha and vegetable"

Lovely, what you cooked in vegetable?

"Cauliflower, potatoes and tomato mixed vegetable."

Well done. What a nice dinner.

"I have cooked rice and lentil soup too. I know you like soup much more than simple vegetable. That's why I prepared specially lentil soup for you."

How you manage to prepare all these in such small time?

I think I was out for one hour and fifteen minutes only.

"I used all four stoves for cooking. One stove for rice second for soup and third for vegetable. I prepared flour for pararha and cut onion for pakoras. In the frying pan I made paratha, then poured oil and fried pakoras on fourth."

Lovely you made all very quick. I never realized that you became a good cook.

"I was frying Pakoras when you park the car and climbing stairs. It is all because of you. You trained me and given important tips how to cook fast. I implemented those tips and cooked dinner fast."

We enjoyed dinner. It was delicious. After dinner we gone in bed and slept.

"I am on evening duty next day that is Monday. Do not disturb me early in the morning. You proceed with your regular chore."

I got up early and gone for morning walk. I took bath and enter prayer room. I found she was praying. I started prayer and when I finished she call me.

"You come my darling breakfast is ready. I am waiting for you."

I dressed and came on table for breakfast. She served toast, butter, cereal, milk and hot tea in the breakfast. I ate breakfast and getting ready for office.

"What you will take in lunch?"

Please cook anything light easy to digest. Do not prepare heavy and oily food in lunch. I told her while starting my car. I went to work.

We met in lunch. She cooked rice and soup mixed with leafy vegetable and tomatoes. She cooked all in her flat but brought in my flat before lunch.

"Hi love! Wash your hand and fresh up. Lunch is ready."

All right darling I am coming and join you. Please serve lunch in the plate. She served lunch in the plates. We enjoyed lunch and gone for a snap after lunch.

I was getting ready for duty after washing my face.

"Here is your cup of tea."

Darling you are taking so much care of me. Thanks for all this.

"I am not only your love or girlfriend. I am you spiritual wife too. A wife must take care of her husband or life partner. So I am taking care of you."

I thanked her and left for work after tea. She left my flat after me as she has evening duty.

[5]

ONE DAY IN LUNCH I rang her. She was in sound sleep. She lifted phone after so many ring and said hello.

What are you doing?

"I am sleeping. Are you calling from work?"

No, I am back to home. What about your lunch, did you finished?

"No, I haven't cooked lunch today. I am tired. Please let me sleep. I don't want to take lunch."

I am cooking lunch you come and join me.

"I am sleeping."

You come take lunch and sleep.

"Please excuse me today. I am completely tired. If I come something may take place. We can't control then."

No nothing will take place. You come and join in lunch.

"If so then I am coming."

I cooked mix vegetable and backed bread. It was easy to cook and keep busy also. It took just thirty minutes and lunch was ready.

"Hi I am here now. You have disturbed my sleep and rest,"

If you are hungry how you can sleep and take rest? You finish your lunch and then sleep.

"All right I am at dining table please bring lunch."

I brought food on table and served her. I took my plate, said grace and started lunch.

We finished lunch and as usual took rest.

She was sleeping. I make tea dressed up, took tea and left for work.

I back from the work at five. She had already left my house. I had gone for evening walk. We met after my evening walk.

"I have prepared dinner. Hope you will like it."

I haven't disliked the food. If it is prepared by beloved one its taste get multiplied. I mean it becomes hundred times tastier than its normal taste. I am going for shower.

"No, let me do my work. Come inside bathroom."

She shaved my genital area and then lay down and asked me to shave her genital area.

"Now our genital area is cleaned no hairs. This you want."

I said yes and then we both took shower, after that performed prayer.

"I have prepared two cups of coffee. Please come and join me."

We took hot coffee and listen radio. Later we chitchat family matters and then gone for dinner.

We watched movie which I rented for two days. I fell asleep while she was not. She had nice sleep in day time. Hence she was watching movie.

"Are you sleeping? She asked me swiftly and kissed me. Let us enjoy sex. Now our genital area is hairless!"

We should enjoy swinging sex today, a new pose to have good sex but little risky.

"It is ok no problem let us do it."

I stood naked against a beam projected in the wall so that much leg room available for her. I asked her to cross her fingers and put palm behind my neck and hang on.

"I cross my finger like this (shown to me) and put my palm behind your neck."

Yes, it is ok. I crossed my finger and hold her buttock on my palm pulled little her up.

"Let me put cock inside you hold me please."

She aligned her pussy against my cock and gave a gentle push.

"Yes it is fully inside. Today it is hard and tighter why?"

You shaved it and we had no sex for few days.

"I am hanging on your neck. It is fine."

It is fine. Keep your feet against wall and help me when I swing you.

"You mean I should stretch my leg against wall and fold it when you swing me?"

Yes, it will automatically take place even you do not want to do. Are you ready—I asked her?

"Yes I am. She replied."

I little bend down, holding her buttock on my palm I took away her from dick and then bring back to normal position. I did this twice.

"Hey it is giving more pleasure. On stretching my leg, cock is fully out but only front of cock remain engaged in pussy giving peculiar sensation that forces me to fold my leg quick. On folding the legs it goes fully in, I can't say how deep it goes in but giving more pleasure. I am getting more pleasure in this pose but may ejaculate quick,"

She was swinging by pushing her leg against wall. Her total weight was on my hand. She was in comfortable position and enjoying sex.

I asked her to be careful and tell me before you ejaculate.

"I shall tell you but you please take care, do not put semen inside to make me pregnant. Otherwise we shall be in big trouble and get bad name too."

I shall comply with you.

"I am swinging and enjoying. Let me swing fast keep your hand under my buttock and help me in swinging please."

She was swinging fast and finally we both ejaculated.

We both gone in bathroom and cleaned the semen which was fallen on my legs. I hold her and came in bed and sleep.

I told her still much more postures are there to enjoy. Kamashutra described eighty four poses of the healthy sex postures in the book.

"I shall enjoy all postures with you my love. You make my stay here meaningful and pleasure."

We slept holding each other under blanket till morning.

Air conditioning was on at full swing gives more pleasure to us to hold each other. Her round and beautiful breast against my chest was giving tremendous pleasure.

I asked her—your breast is so tight like virgin girl. You have not breast fed your children?

"I had taken care during breast feeding. I always fed babies sleeping in the bed or holding them near breast. I have not allowed babies to pull the breast."

So, you know techniques how to feed babies keeping breast intact at the same time.

"Yes, being in the hospital I consulted doctors used medicine and cream to keep my breast tight and intact."

Do you feel bad when I rub your breast?

"No, it gives me pleasure when you rub gently. In fact I get more sensations and temptation for sex when you rub it. When you kiss my nipple and hold under your lips. I get excited more vigorously."

These are points to seduce more sexual desire in women. If I touch breast more gently then also you will feel sensations. A peculiar type of sensation, which will vibrate your whole body and you tempt for great sex. If you want to experience it, I'll do that next time.

"No, today it is too much. I shall back from my night duty then we shall enjoy again."

You mean after three days.

"No, not three days, I am going today night duty and next morning I shall back. Whole the day I shall be in your flat for washing my clothes and ironing my dress. If you have clothes for laundry leave them near washing machine. I shall wash and iron them too."

Then it is ok. Today you have night duty.

"Yes I am. What is time now?"

It is half pass nine.

"Then I must go to my flat and get ready for duty."

What time hospital van will come to pick you up?

"Van may come half pass ten to quarter to eleven."

Still you have one hour time. Since you are tired I am giving you a glass of warm milk.

"You will make me fat."

What? A glass of milk will make you fat.

"The way I am eating here in your home my body weight is increasing."

You weigh yourself today and tell me how much your weight increased.

"Fine, I shall weight myself in hospital and let you know."

She finished glass of milk and left for duty with warm kisses.

I went in bed and sleep nicely.

I got call at twelve midnight.

"This is me darling. Sorry to disturb you."

Tell me why you called me.

"I just wanted to talk to you. There is nothing to do today so I thought I must talk to you instead of chitchat with girls here."

We chitchat for fifteen minutes. She told me a patient has come. She is going to attend her.

"Bye for now."

I slept and got up at half pass five in the morning, prepared tea and gone for morning walk. I met old guys walking on the road. They usually sit down after walking a kilo meter and stop me also.

I decided to go for long walk like in the evening but time was less. I took short brisk walk and back to my flat.

I got ready for work after taking my breakfast.

[6]

I T WAS FRIDAY EVENING PEOPLE were enjoying weekend. I also planned to enjoy weekend. She has morning duty on Saturday this was only hurdle. I purchased a case of beer, green salad, case of coca-cola and popcorn packets from super market after office hours. So I was late to reach home.

When I entered in my flat I got a call.

I lifted phone and said hello.

"Hi darling it's me why you are so late to reach home."

I was busy at work.

"I rang you in office but you were not there. No one lifted phone."

I was in airline office there was some problem with reservation terminal.

"It is seven in the evening I am coming now and then will talk."

Give me just fifteen minutes please.

"Why? What is there which you can't do in front of me?"

There is surprise for you, which I can't do in front of you.

"I am eager to know now. I can't stop. Please allow me to come."

I was keeping beer in fridge at least six cans so that we can enjoy well. Ok you are welcome.

I left rest cans and gone in bathroom for shower.

She knocked door and took her key open it. She was in the hall now. She was having food packets in her hand. She left all food packets on table and came to me.

I asked her a cup of tea.

"Sure. Let me warm water and prepare tea."

She prepared tea while I prayed God.

We were sipping tea and talking mean while rain started.

"It is good combination tea and rain. Is it not?"

It is. Today is start of weekend and people are enjoying. Let us also enjoy.

"I have got my duty exchanged. I am going evening duty tomorrow. One of my staff has party tomorrow evening. She requested for duty exchange and I agreed."

Well you have done nice thing. It means we can enjoy whole the night.

"Where we are going?"

We are not going anywhere. We are staying in this flat. Party will start at sharp eight and what time it will finish I can't say.

"How many people are joining the party?"

Eleven, eleven people are coming to the party.

"I have cooked food for both of us. How we are going to manage? Only fifteen minutes left to start the party."

Don't worry! I have something will manage.

"Let me go home I have no proper dress. I am in night gown. What people will think about me? You must have told me before."

Don't worry I am telling you. I shall manage all. Now you can't go see heavy rain.

"Then how people will come?"

They are coming in their car. I saw her face. She was feeling uncomfortable.

Can you bring glasses and keep the cups in the tub.

"I shall clean cups and bring glasses on the table."

She arranged twelve glasses, paper napkins and then asked me.

"What you are going to offer in drink?

I have something in the fridge. Can you open fridge please.

"Beer! Then let them come. What you will give them to eat with drink?"

Pop corns will go with drink.

"You want me to prepare Pakoras also."

No they will take pop corns only with drink. What about you?

"It is my favourite. I am happy with this."

Pour beer in the two glasses then I'll tell you. She filled two glasses.

"Here is beer in two glasses."

I took one and sat on sofa and called her to come with her glass and sit side by me.

She brought her drink and sit side by me.

"Now tell me."

I am telling truth. Only you and I are in this party no one else.

"I know that you will not call any one between us."

We were drinking and eating pop corns. I asked her what you have cooked in dinner.

"I prepared Spinach Parathas and vegetable."

Well it is nice for the season. Do you know that it will rain today?

"Every day it rains nothing new. Sometime it rains in the morning some times in the evening or night."

We finished four cans of beer two can each. I asked her should we go for one-one more.

"No, not one more, we will take half-half."

Will you serve darling? She got up, took beer from fridge and poured in the glasses.

"Here is your drink."

We cross our hand and sip drink from other's glasses.

"This will increase our love." She said.

Sure, let us finish then will go for dinner. She finished drink.

"I am going bathroom then come back and serve dinner."

I also finished my drink and arranged plates on the table.

She came back from bathroom warmed food, brought on table and served.

We said grace and enjoyed dinner. Dinner was very delicious. I told her food was very nice.

"Your appreciation makes me happy."

Really it is nice. I am not just appreciated you.

"Thanks for complement."

I served vanilla Ice Cream in cups after dinner.

Suddenly I saw clock. It is midnight now.

"It is bed time. Let us go in the bed."

We went in the bedroom. She arranged bed while I was in bathroom. I came in the bed and fell asleep.

"Are you sleeping?"

Yes I am.

"We are not going to play today."

We shall play after taking little rest. You chitchat with me.

I hold her in my arms kissed her at cheek. We do not know when but both slept without playing.

I got up at half pass five in the morning. I wake her up and started play. I asked her to be on her knees on the bed and lift her buttock up. I asked her to grab pillow and put under her chest and rest in that pose (Dog pose). I kept my leg inside her legs, inserted cock in her pussy and pushed. I rub her breasts in this posture. She was much excited. Then I hold her waist by my both the hands pulled against my cock while pushing hard in her pussy. Cock was fully in. I speeded up the action.

"Yeeeh, how much you want to push. It has gone deep in. Can you take out and put back again. I am feeling hard in me."

I comply with her and then I keep on pumping. She was enjoying the moment and posture. I was exhausted and ejaculated. I dropped semen on her back and asked her to make legs straigh. I pushed her down and removed pillow. She was completely on the bed and I was lie on her back.

"What you did? You dropped semen on my back. I am feeling uneasy. Let me clean."

Wait you can't go. If you go all, bed sheet and floor of bedroom will be dirty. I am bringing towel for you to clean. I was still on her back in the same position few minutes and enjoying. I was getting pleasure. Later I got up and brought towel. I cleaned her back with towel. Then I asked her to put it in the laundry and go to washroom and wash with water.

"It was giving pleasure but I can't tolerate your weight."

That I did to avoid semen should not go inside to make you pregnant.

"You would have dropped on the bed sheet."

Then I would have not got much pleasure. You have noticed my cock was against your back while semen was coming out with force. That was real pleasure. It was pulsating and semen coming out.

"It appears to me that something hot liquid falling on my back. I really feel hot and uneasy. Let me come up. I want to enjoy."

First I want to wash mine otherwise left over semen may cause some problem to you. She came with me and washed mine with clean water. I washed semen fell on her back. We took some sweet and gone in the bed.

"Let me climbed up."

I lie down face up. She was sitting on my thigh, took position and set cock to her pussy.

"Let me take your cock in. Oh aah it is fully in now."

She gave strong thrust twice and enjoying rhythmic up down fast. She pushed hard quickly few time and then ejaculated. She lied on my chest and rested on it.

"I am exhausted now. I shall clean your genital area. I fell off make your genital area wet. Lots of fluid came out from vagina. Let me have rest for moment."

Why not darling you can take rest. I hold her hard. We were tired and slept in this position till morning eight o'clock without cleaning.

"I made bed sheet dirty. I shall wash in the machine."

Darling now bed sheet is fully dirty. I want to enjoy once before I start my day.

"No, it is too much for the day. You get up I'll put dirty clothes for laundry."

I was in bath room while she took all dirty clothes for laundry in the machine. She came in bath room. I was ready for shower.

"You go out for a while please. It is urgent."

I came out after ten minutes she called me and gave shower to me. We applied soap on each other's body.

We both took shower and had sex under shower while soap was on our body. It was very slippery. We enjoyed it very well.

"This completes morning session as you desired. I took bed sheet for wash. Later I realized you may be angry because I denied sex that time."

I was really tired after sex under shower. She cooked breakfast for us.

"Come breakfast is ready. Let us have it."

I asked her to warm two glasses of milk so that we become fresh and get more energy.

"I know after milk you are going for sex again."

No, Promise I shall not go for sex again.

"I shall bring warm milk please wait."

She warmed milk and brought it in glasses on the table.

"Here is milk for you."

I brought chocolate. It was kept in the fridge. I gave her to eat before she took milk.

"Milk and chocolate is very good combination. It will give us more energy."

Yes it will. We require it otherwise cooking will not be possible. We eat breakfast, took milk and later tea.

She kept cups and plates in wash basin and gone to restroom.

"We look fresh now. Breakfast was full of energy. I looked in mirror no sign of tiredness on the face. Thanks for this."

You are welcome my love. I have kept everything you have to just search them.

"What you want me to search now?"

Come I shall tell you. She come closure to me. I hold tightly and kissed her. I asked go and see your face in the mirror. She saw her face in the mirror.

"What you did? You make mark on my cheek. You not kissed me but cut my cheek."

I say sorry to her and asked if blood has come out.

"See marks of your teeth on my cheek. Blood is not come out but marks are visible."

I applied cream on her face and put little face power so that mark may not be visible. I asked her to check face again and tell me. She checked face in the mirror.

"Yes it is fine now."

Are you happy?

"Yes I am. Now let us go out for marketing."

We shall go but not now. It is 11 AM all the people would be in the market.

"So what, I'll get down from car and do my shopping. I shall be away from you in supermarkets."

We got ready and started car for market.

This was first time when I gone in the market with her during day time when all our community people were shopping.

She did her shopping. I purchased some readymade clothes. I purchased a white knitted dress for her. It was really beautiful.

"What you have purchased—She asked me."

I have purchased shirt and some other clothes.

"I had no soft drink at my flat so I purchased some."

Where is that?

"I asked shopkeeper to keep in your car."

You please check if it is kept or not.

"He already kept. I have seen it."

Where you want to go now?

"Let us go hill side. We'll enjoy cool breeze and pass some time under trees."

You want to go hill side in this rain.

"Yes I want to enjoy rain in the forest."

I started car and reached another Super Market. I purchased a crate of beer, potato chips, Nair cream, Ponds cold cream, deodorant, perfumes etc.

"Let us go quick some people are coming in this mall—She murmured."

I started my car and soon I was on the road leading to forest. Within fifteen minutes I reached jungle. I knew some sites which are pleasant, surrounded by trees, having good plane ground covered by green carpet of grass. I stopped car under tree and sit outside with beer and chips and enjoying rain. We spend one hour there and took two cans of bear. We enjoyed rain and were wet.

"I feel sleepy. Let us go back to home."

I started car driving slowly because of rain and bad road. We reached home in thirty minutes. She rushed in bathroom and changed her dress.

"I shall prepare quick lunch mean while you change."

I changed my dress and put all wet clothes in machine for laundry.

She cooked noodle and prepared soup. She kept all on dining table and asked me to bring plates and spoons.

"I am hungry please come quick."

Yes darling I am coming with plates and spoons. She served noodles and soup. We ate lunch then gone in bed for the rest.

"I am feeling cold. Please switched off air conditioner, hold me in your arms and sleep."

I am coming wait. I pulled rag on her, switched off air conditioner, hold her in my arms and slept.

I got up at 6 O'clock in the evening, woke her up also. She prepared tea for us. We both enjoyed evening tea.

What duty you have today? I asked her.

"I am off today. Tomorrow I will go for morning duty."

[7]

EXT DAY I GAVE HER what I had purchased. All these things are for you darling. Nair (hair removing cream), Ponds cold cream, and dress all were in a bag I handed over to her.

"Why you have spent so much on me? I am happy with your company and your help in entertaining me out of the way. Please keep these for your wife."

She does not wear theses dresses. Can you please wear it? Let me see how you look in this dress. She open bag and saw dress.

"I shall have shower in the evening and then I put on this beautiful dress."

That would be fine. Before you go shower apply Nair cream on the private part, follow instructions on the label and then took shower.

"You always want hair less?"

Yes darling I want.

"Let both of us go for this. I shall apply on you and then on me."

She pulled me in the bathroom and applied cream on me.

She applied on her later. We took shower. We laughed— hairless genitals. We prayed God.

She applied deodorant, adored in white dress, wears perfumed and sprayed on me too.

You look beautiful in this white dress. Let me put mascara on your face so that no one cast sinister eye on you.

"Thanks for comments. I am really thankful to you for giving me nice dress. I shall remember whole of my life this."

Darling what I have done for you is nothing. You said—you are my wife now (a spiritual wife). A dress is not enough. I would have given you much more.

"Your love is more than anything for me. You keep this going. Just promise me you will not deny in any circumstances till you are here. This will be great gift for me."

I am with you and will remain yours don't worry. I shall try my best to keep this union going on.

"I trust you. Let me do my work. I shall prepare dinner. What shall I cook?"

Now you select some vegetable, lentil soup and rice as usual. I shall bake chapattis.

It was raining so I postponed my evening walk.

"I shall cook green peas, potatoes mixed vegetable, rice and lentil soup. Will it be ok?"

Of course yes darling. When you finished cooking tell me for chapattis.

"Sure. I'll inform you."

I prepared drink for both of us, offered one to her and started enjoying drink. After some time she came to me from kitchen.

"My cooking is over. You can take over kitchen."

I started preparing chapattis. In few minutes I baked chapattis. Now dinner was ready but we were still drinking.

"It is ten O'clock. Let me serve dinner."

She served dinner in the plates. We ate dinner and then gone for bed.

I asked her to sleep in new dress.

"Yes I knew you will ask this. Do you want to make dirty this dress?"

No, I shall enjoy with you in this dress but no make dirty.

"It is not possible. You want to enjoy and dress will not be dirty."

It is possible.

"How?"

I will tell you later. We both laughed.

"You are very naughty today."

You look very cute in this dress. I am not kidding.

I hold her in my arms, kissed and took her in the bed.

I asked her to lie down face up. I sit in between her legs keeping them on my shoulder. She took my dick in her pussy and we were started enjoying sex.

"I want to climb on you. Once you finish let me know."

Sure, I shall let you know. I was enjoying and I exhausted in few minutes. Her genital area was full of fluids. She cleaned mine and later her with towel.

After a gap of fifteen minutes, I invited her to come up on me. She climbed and put my cock in her pussy. She pulled me and asked to hold her at shoulder.

"Can you please put pillow under you buttock?"

I grab one and kept under my buttock.

"It is fine now. She was holding my shoulder and sliding back and forth on cock. She was speedy and crying oh ooh, in the pleasure and then ejaculated. I am exhausted please hold me."

I hold her in arms and turn a side. I gave her safe side in the bed.

"Today it is tight and hard. You have not ejaculated yet or what?"

It was my second round. Second round generally stay longer that is reason why I have not ejaculated and dick is hard and tight.

"I am yours you enjoy now, please go ahead."

You are tired. I am bringing something to make you fresh and energetic please wait a moment.

I gave her chocolate bar and took myself too. I gave her warm milk also after fifteen minutes.

"Where is your glass—she asked me?"

I am coming with mine.

"No unless I see your glass I am not going to take milk."

I brought mine and shown to her—here is mine. We both had milk.

"I am ready now if you want to enjoy please."

Sure, I enjoyed sex again this time it was more vigorous.

I ejaculated this time along with her. Her vaginal area was wet because lots of our discharges came out from her vagina.

"Now I want to sleep. Let me clean it."

She cleaned with soft towel mine first and then her own.

I hold her in my arms, kissed her and slept till morning. We got up after alarm buzzed.

It was half pass five in the morning. You get ready for duty.

"I am going in bathroom. You go for morning walk."

I prepared tea. She came from bathroom and we took tea. She left for her flat and me for morning walk.

[8]

ONE DAY I COULD NOT come for lunch due to emergency work in the office. I back from duty in the evening and was resting. She came in my flat.

"Where were you in the lunch—she asked me? I was calling but no reply."

I was busy in the office in an emergency work. I took Chinese in lunch today from restaurant.

"You look tired today."

Yes, continuous work without proper lunch and rest make me tired.

"I shall prepare some snacks and hot tea for you so that you feel fresh."

She prepared a dish from semolina known as Upma. It contains onion, mustard seed, tomato, chilli, salt, cooking oil and water. It is very tasty dish and easy to cook. It takes just 10 minutes to prepare dish.

"Here is your snacks. I am bringing tea. Please start—she said to me."

I started eating snacks. She brought cup of tea and a glass of water for me. Later she brought her snacks and tea and joined me on table.

I asked her—you have taken very little snacks.

"I had my lunch in hospital. I took some biscuits when I came home after work. This is too much for me. I am taking this to give you company."

I finished tea and wanted to go for evening walk.

"You look tired take rest. Please do not go for evening walk today."

No, I am fresh now. Let me go for evening walk otherwise friends will feel I am sick and they will visit me at the home. Do you want them to visit me?

"No, you are right. You may go for evening walk but come quick and alone. Don't bring any friend with you."

I shall be back soon and alone. You cook dinner for us.

"I shall cook it. You please go now. It is getting late."

Are you angry?

"No, I am not angry. Please carry on."

I had gone for evening walk. I met a friend and gone for long walk. I came late.

Sorry darling I am late. I met a friend and gone for long walk.

"I have kept lime water you take it while resting."

Where are you?

"I am taking shower darling."

I sat on sofa sipping glass of lime water. I slept on sofa while waiting her to come out of shower.

She performed prayer and came to hall where I was sleeping. She kissed me.

"Wake up my love. Go for shower now. Dinner is ready, eat then go for bed early today and sleep."

I got up, took shower, performed prayer and was ready for dinner.

"I shall serve dinner. Please bring plates and pickle."

She served dinner and we both started eating after grace.

"Why you are very quiet today?"

I am tired and took long walk that's why I slept on sofa. I am not fully awake. Thank you for wake me up. I am feeling sleepy.

"You finish dinner and go to bed."

We finished dinner. I was in bath room she arranged my bed. I went straight into bed. She warmed milk for us.

"Here is your milk you finish it. Hurry up."

I took glass of milk and sipped.

"I am going to my flat."

No, you will stay here.

"No, let me go please. It is not late just 10 O'clock in night."

I am not looking at time. I am asking you to stay with me.

"I shall keep you disturbing in the night. You have to go at work in the morning. So better you take rest."

I hold and pulled her in the bed. Now I am wake up. You can't leave me alone.

"I am in your arms but I want you to take rest today. I hope you understand me."

Yes I understand what you trying to tell me. I shall sleep holding you in my arms all the night.

"I can't sleep like this. When I am away from you, I sleep alone. In your arms I can't sleep unless I have sex."

Do you want sex right now or can we do it in the early morning?

"I want right now. Once sex session is over we can sleep peacefully."

All right let us go for sex then.

She stripped off me. I also removed all her clothes. I asked her to enjoy the sex the way she wants.

"I shall come on you just wait a moment."

She holds my dick and aligned properly in her pussy and pushed hard.

"It is very tight today. It is hard like iron rod. I am feeling pain. Let me re-adjust."

She took out, aligned properly and then taken it in her pussy.

"Now it is fine. It has reached deep in. She was in action, speedy and asked me to rub her tits."

I rubbed her tits, she pushes hard and screaming too.

She was fast today in enjoying sex. Number of occasions she pushed hard taking dick fully in and cried—oh ooh . . . yeah.

"I ejaculated and exhausted now. Please hold me in your arms. Let me lie down on your chest."

I found unusual tiredness in her. Later I saw bed sheet was wet. I switched light on. Bed sheet was dirty with red spots due to heavy bleeding.

You know darling, it seems you got period. Bed sheet is full of blood stains. Let me remove it.

"No, you also enjoy before we change the bed sheet. I shall take care of it."

You want me to enjoy sex in this condition?

"Yes, it is very good to enjoy sex in this condition. Come on and have sex now."

I asked her to lie down on the bed face up. I hold her both legs on my shoulder. She set cock to her pussy then I pushed. I was enjoying sex with speed. She was feeling pleasure. At the peak point she holds me firmly. I ejaculated inside her pussy.

I asked her why she allowed me to ejaculate inside. She may get pregnant.

"You don't worry. This is safe period pregnancy is not possible during menstruation."

Her vagina was full of semen and blood mixed fluid. All was coming out from vagina and falling on bed sheet.

I asked her to clean the pussy as she was still bleeding. She cleaned with towel.

"Come and enjoy sex again. I am feeling pleasure of sex in this condition."

I back from washroom and took chocolates for us. After few minutes of eating chocolate we were again ready for sex. This time we enjoyed sex for longer time and finally ejaculated inside her pussy.

"Please ejaculate inside. Warm fluid inside vagina gives a peculiar pleasure and feeling of oneness. Also it is safe period for me. Nothing will happen you please drop semen inside for the duration of period. I mean from today till seven days."

I firmly pushed cock inside and I got pleasure while ejaculating inside her. It was pulsating. She was counting how many time I ejaculated.

"It was eight to nine pulsating I could count. You dropped inside. I am happy today. What about you?"

I also enjoyed much particularly ejaculating inside your vagina gave me more pleasure. I was feeling cock has fully in and there was no room for it to go further. I found real pleasure during pulsations while ejaculating.

"Sleep now in dirty condition. Bed sheet was full of blood and semen."

I can't sleep like this.

"You want me to get up and clean?"

No, you change the bed sheet. I will clean and wash my genital.

She got up removed bed sheet. I hold and took her in bath room. She was much tired.

"Let me urinate first and then will clean."

She urinated and cleaned her pussy with water and applied little dettol and finally rinsed with water.

I also urinated and she cleaned my dick with water. She holds my cock and pushed foreskin back and cleaned properly by removing red bloods accumulated near ring of the penis. Later she applied dettol and rinsed with water.

"It is warm inside me."

I am also feeling warm. It is due to dettol. I gave cold cream to apply on her pussy.

She applied on her pussy and on my cock too.

I gave another piece of chocolate to her and I took one.

"Can I get a glass of water?"

Sure, I gave her water. Then we make bed with fresh bed sheet. Let us sleep now.

"I do not have napkin with me."

I gave a soft towel to use it in place of napkin.

"It is too big I can't take this."

I make two pieces and asked her it should be ok.

"Make two pieces in each one again."

It will be then too small.

"No. It would be fine and fit properly."

I made two pieces again and gave her.

"I will take one on and keep other pieces in case I need in night any time."

Sure, I am keeping all under your pillow so that you can take when required.

We both slept holding her in my arms. I kissed her on cheek and gently rubbed her breast.

"No, please do not do anything otherwise urge of sex will reactivated and this bed sheet will also become dirty."

I said sorry and stopped rubbing her breast.

We both slept until 7 AM in the morning. I had switched off alarm that's why it did not buzz at 5. 30 AM

I was getting ready for work. She prepared breakfast and we were on table eating our breakfast. I asked her duty.

"I am having evening duty today. I shall cook lunch at my flat and bring here during lunch."

It would be fine for me. I started for work and purchased a pack of napkin for her from supermarket. Counter girl asked me is it for your wife.

Yes, it is for my wife. I replied.

You take other brand that is good.

Can you please help me selecting good one?

Counter girl gave me good quality napkin's pack. I paid and started for home.

"Why you became late today?"

I was purchasing napkins for you.

"Anyone noticed that you are buying napkins?"

No I purchased after office hour when no one in the supermarket.

"Thanks for this. Please wash your hand I am serving you lunch."

I gone in washroom and cleaned my hand. She served lunch and we were eating lunch.

"Did you enjoy sex with your wife when she was in menstruation?"

No, she has not allowed me during her menses.

"If you have sex with her during period she will feel easy bleeding and then no fear of blood dropping."

I shall try when she is with me and having period. We finished our lunch and took little rest.

"I shall come in the night after my work. Please do not sleep."

I'll not sleep and even I slept you have key. You can open and come in my flat.

"I shall come from road side because van stop on the road. I do not have key for that side door. It will be easy for me to come in quick."

I will keep busy myself to avoid sleep.

She gave a cup of tea then I started for my duty.

"I shall change napkin then go to my flat."

As you wish house is yours. I went to work.

In the night, I was awake till 11:30 PM. She had not turned up. I was upset. I rang her home number but no response. I was sure that she has not returned from work.

I heard knocking sound on the door. I saw she was standing at the door. I open the door for her.

"I became late as tyre of the van got flat. Second van deployed to take us from the site. I am having headache. What is time now?"

It is quarter pass twelve in the night. You change and wash your face. I will serve you dinner.

"No, I had my dinner in the hospital."

I was waiting for you and have not taken dinner yet.

"What you were doing?"

I was waiting you and drinking beer so that we both take dinner together.

"I am coming on the table for dinner to give you company just wait."

I was on the dining table. She fresh up and joined me on dinner.

"I shall serve dinner."

She served me dinner in the plate and took herself too. We both finished dinner while chit-chat about work for the day.

"Work was tiresome much rush and then on the way van got flat tyre and make us tired waiting other van to come from hospital and drop us home."

We took hot milk and gone in the bed room.

"Today there was rush in the hospital. I am tired. I did not take dinner there. A case of accident came and boy was dead. I did stitches on him and feeling sad for him."

This is part of your job. Do not feel sad. You have not done anything bad to the boy. Sympathy to his family is appreciated.

"His family members were crying. I feel cry too."

This is natural. You calm down and have rest.

"Thank you so much."

I applied pain balm on her head so that she can get sleep quick.

"What you applied on my fore head?"

I applied pain balm darling. This will give you little relief from headache and you can sleep well.

"Can you hold me and pull over blanket?"

I shall put blanket over you. You sleep now. I will not hold you otherwise your sleep get disturbed.

"No, once you hold me in your arm I will feel secured and sleep quickly."

I gone in the bed and hold her in my arms. Since she was in bad mood and tired. It is my duty to be sympathetic to her and help her to sleep well. After few minutes she slept. I also slept till morning. I got up on alarm at half pass five.

I was ready for morning walk leaving her in the bed. I took long walk in the morning and returned after one hour.

I took bath and gone in prayer room. She was in prayer room performing prayer. I joined her and performed prayer.

She finished prayer and started preparing breakfast. I asked her when she got up.

"Just 30 minutes before you came I got up."

I took rest after walk and gone to bath room. I did not check bed room I thought you are still sleeping.

"Here is milk, bran, toast, butter and bowls. I am coming with tea."

Shall I start darling?

"Yes my love you start. I am joining you soon."

We finished breakfast. I got ready for work. She had day off today.

"I will go to my flat and have rest."

I was in the office. My telephone buzzed once only. I know she is calling me. Later phone buzzed again. I lifted phone. May I help you?

"Yes please. Why you not say my darling or my love as usually you say to me?"

I think you have got wrong number. I am not dealing with this problem. Please check number before you call. I replied her on phone.

"I know it means someone is in the office with you."

Yes you are right.

"Shall I disconnect now?"

Yes please. She kissed and kept receiver on the hook.

We met in the lunch. She had cooked lunch in her flat and brought to mine. I was changing and getting ready for lunch. She came to help and removed my shirt.

"Shall we go for lunch? It is ready."

Of course yes darling.

"I am serving please come quick"

I am joining just a minute. We started lunch and had some chitchat and then gone for rest.

"I need something."

What do you need?

"I want to have sex now—she said."

I think it would be better in the night. Today you are off. We shall enjoy in the night and in good manner. Lunch time is short, after sex we will not get time to have proper rest. I shall feel uneasy at work and people will notice my sluggishness at work. Do you agree with me?

"Yes I am in agreement with you."

Let us have some rest. You may prepare tea for us after few minutes.

"Yes I shall do that. Can I offer coffee today?"

Yes my love I accept anything you offer me.

"I wish to give you kiss. I mean kiss you."

Fine you can. She kissed me. I took snap then fresh up, got ready for duty.

"Here is your cup darling."

She gave cup of coffee to me. We finished coffee. I started for work. I was busy at work lots of complain from different offices for their computer terminals. I checked and found it was due to cable problem. I went to attend problem at customer nearby a supermarket and rain started. I thought to purchase something from market because I can't go to car park in the rain. I purchased cheese, potato chips, peas, green vegetables and a bottle of whisky.

Rain slowed down at half pass six then I manage to reach car park. I started car came on the road. Road was flooded, lots of cars stopped on the road because of heavy rain. I drove slowly and manage to reach my flat.

I open door and kept things on table and gone straight in bathroom to change and fresh up. I went in kitchen to make a cup of tea. I found she was near door and completely wet. I open door and asked her to go in bathroom to have shower and change her dress.

"No you come first to my flat. My flat is locked and all keys are inside."

I am going to open your flat and bring back all keys. Mean while you go bathroom and fresh up change your dress.

"I shall fresh up. I am getting cold and shivering now."

You take hot water bath and then take hot tea I am coming. I took umbrella and gone to her flat to open door. I took some spare keys and a knife with me. I managed to open her flat with the help of knife, locked her flat, took her key bunch and back to my flat.

You look beautiful in this dress—I commented. She was in my kurta and payjama, both milky white. Her hair was scattered and few came on her face increasing her beauty.

"Thanks for nice remarks. You know what happened. I left your flat after you went to work. I was sleeping in my flat. I heard lots of sound. I came out and found coconuts were falling on the roof from trees due to heavy wind and rain. I saw few green coconuts on the ground. I went to collect them while heavy wind closed door of my flat. I left all keys inside my flat.

I was in problem and could not go in others flat to give you call in this dress. I came to your flat thrice to see you but your car was not there. I went back to my flat and was wet. I am feeling cold. Can I get a cup of coffee?"

Sure, give me few minutes. I prepared two cups of coffee and offer a cup to her. I gave potato chips with coffee. She took some and finished coffee.

"I am shivering please give me blanket I am going in bed room."

She was in the bed I covered her with blanket. Do you want to sleep?

"No I want to be warmed up. I am feeling cold. Please come in the bed."

I shall come in give me some time. I went in kitchen and fried pakoras, cut cheese pieces, and make two drinks of whisky in soda without ice.

Darling I am here with something.

"I don't want anything. I want you to come in the bed, hold me and warm me up. Why are you late today?"

I was attending problem at a customer's office in the market then rain started. I was unable to go in the car park due to heavy rain. Rain slowed down at 6:30 then I managed to go to car park and started for home.

"I came three times to your flat and gone back that's why I get cold."

You want me in the bed or will take something which I prepared for us. She looked at glass and plate contains pakoras.

"You have prepared something is nice. I shall take that later first you come in the bed."

I was in the bed keeping drinks and pakoras on side table.

"Hold me in your arms, kiss me, and let me have your dick."

I hold her tight kissed and she hold my dick in her hand. It was raining heavily, climate was quite cold. I tighten my hold.

"Let me remove kurta and payjama."

Let me kiss darling then whatever you want to do you do.

"Just kissing will not help. Let us remove our clothes."

She removed her clothes and mine.

"Now kiss my nipples, rub my breasts and let me set cock at correct position"

I kissed her nipples and grabbed her breasts while pushed hard my cock in her pussy.

"No, she cried it is not set properly yet please wait."

She set the cock correctly, pushed herself and took my dick fully in the pussy."

"You go down let me up I want to get warm."

She was up and speedy she was murmuring something. I asked what you are saying.

"Nothing, Don't talk at this moment. Fucking and talking can't go together. I shall tell you later. Let me finish my work first."

I tighten it, holding her hip and pulling towards cock.

"Aaa . . . . ah, it is hard and full of joy. Let me enjoy. I shall take few more minutes."

I was exited much and nearing ejaculation. I warned her any moment I may ejaculate in her.

"No, no please hold few minutes."

I am trying but not guaranteeing any moment I may fell.

"I am wet. Now your genital area is also wet."

I also ejaculated semen in you.

"Let it be. It is still under safe period."

Do not take chance with safety. You must careful.

"I do take care. I am careful too. Don't worry. Let us go washroom. I shall clean our genital area which is dirty now."

I went first to urinate later she. I collected luck warm water in pot and added few drops of dettol so that its strength is mild.

"Come let me clean you first."

She cleaned her genital area with soap and warm water.

I poured mild dettol on her hand to clean genitals with antiseptic fluid.

Later she cleaned mine. While she was cleaning I got excited. She holds hard, pushed foreskin back and poured warm water on penis. She applied dettol and started foreplay with it. I asked her not to do foreplay if she like let us have another round of intercourse.

"You go on bed I am coming."

I was in bed she perfumed her vagina and came to me on bed.

"I am here with you darling."

Let us take drink before we do something else.

"No you fuck me first then we shall go for drink."

I asked her lie down on bed facing up. I took her legs on my hands and fucked hard. This time I stay in action longer. She was happy and enjoyed sex.

"It is lovely, hard as usual like iron rod, please go fast."

No let me enjoy this moment. I am on apex any moment ejaculation may be.

"I have cleaned just now. It would be nice if you ejaculate outside. If you wish you may drop semen inside also. It is up to you. I am feeling lot more pleasure."

I dropped all semen inside her and rested on her chest. In this position we rested for fifteen minutes.

"Let me go and clean again."

You clean taking water pipe little inside.

"No, I will urinate then clean. I will not use pipe at all."

She cleaned her and called me for cleaning.

We were quite silent after this round. Hunger for the sex of the day was over. Let us enjoy drink now."

Yes, let me heat pakoras again. It is cold now.

"Let us say cheers with drink and cheese then what ever you want to do go and do."

We took drink, said cheers and sipped drink from each other's glasses.

I warmed pakoras in microwave oven and brought in bed room, kept on the table near cheese. Let us enjoy drink now.

We took two pegs of the drinks.

"You were on beer then why switched to whisky?"

You see the climate and season. It is cool so we need hot drink. I was luckily in market so I decided to purchase whisky.

"You decided that you will make romantic night today and enjoy."

Climate asked me to go for whisky. I am really romantic today.

"What you will take in dinner?"

You will prepare dinner.

"Yes, I am ready to cook dinner let me know what you will eat?"

You cook Chickpeas and puree.

I gave her soaked chickpeas and other ingredients to cook.

"Let me cut onions, garlic, tomatoes. Then will mix spices in the mixer before I start cooking dinner."

I'll mix flour for puree mean while.

"That would be fine."

I started kneading flour and make ready for puree.

"I am ready to start cooking."

Ok then start.

She kept pressure cooker on stove, took cooking oil in it. After oil gets heated up she put cumin seed, then chopped onions, garlic, and fried till golden brown. She then added mixed spices and chopped tomato and grated ginger in it. She fried all and then added soaked chickpeas, water and salt to taste. She put lid on the cooker for cooking.

She prepared final drink of the day. She sipped from both the glasses. Taste is same she murmured and gave a glass to me.

"Here is your drink. I have tasted it, hope you like it."

I sipped it is perfect my bar girl. I commented.

"Thanks for comments. I am your bar girl not for others."

Shall I start frying purees now?

"You do it."

You heat oil in pan I am making purees. You have to fry it.

"I am ready darling. Let me put frying pan, oil in it and heat it up."

She cleaned frying pan and dried it. She put pan on stove, poured oil in it.

"Tell me how much oil I should take?"

I was watching and stopped her when required amount of oil was poured.

"What is next?"

Sip your drink till the oil gets heated up.

"See oil is hot now."

I rolled purees and gave her for frying. She put it in hot oil of pan.

"See how it is coming up?"

Turn it upside down and fry both the side. She did that and purees were golden brown.

"Shall I take it out now from pan?"

Yes it is fried nicely take it out and put another. She fried purees and sipped drink also. I was rolling purees and finished my drink too.

"Let us have some rest before we go for dinner."

Fine, I switched on tape recorder and started playing music. Song was her favourite song. She came and hugged me, kissed me and started weeping. I asked her why she is weeping.

"If you had not helped me I decided to put my life to end."

It is very bad thought. You know coward is committing suicide. You are brave. You decided to work overseas and you are here. You should be happy.

"I am happy now. I was much deprived for sex. It was not easy for me without you. I really fell in love with you from the beginning at first site. I think it is true—love at first site. Finally, I manage to get you. If you forgive me for my act then I feel God has pardoned me for my sin."

I have forgiven you. You love me. You offer sex to me. I am able to fulfil your sexual desire. When you told me story of suicide, I feel I did this to save you. I saved you for your innocent kids, loving near and dear.

"Really you extended great help to me and saved my life. I brought sleeping pills with me from hospital. If you had not agreed to my proposals I would had taken all pills in this house for suicide. Morning it would have different story."

I have helped you otherwise according to your plan, on refusal; I would have been in jail for forcing you to take pills.

"Yes, you have helped a lot."

Then forget past and be cheerful.

Let us enjoy music and dinner. I hold her in my arms and kissed. I took her in bathroom and cleaned her face. She fresh up and we both came on dining table for dinner.

"I am serving please wait."

She served dinner in the plates. I said grace and started eating dinner.

"I want you to feed me by your hand and I shall feed you."

As you wish. We ate few nibbles of puree from each other's hand. Then we decided to finish quick as it was 11 PM. We finished dinner took chocolate milk drink and gone in the bed.

We hold each other and enjoyed whole rainy night with great pleasure.

We got up at half pass five after alarms buzzed. "Why alarm buzzed so early?"

It is not early but right time. You get ready and go for duty. Today you are in morning shift.

"My flat is locked."

Yes it is locked but keys are here.

It looks like you are still in dream.

"Yes you are right. I was so tired and shivering from cold in the evening. I am still feeling of same sensations."

Take a cup of hot tea and this tablet you will be fresh again.

"I am going in bathroom."

You go for fresh up and I shall make breakfast and tea for you.

"I shall do that let me fresh up please."

As you wish. Can I prepare tea?

"No, I said no. No means no and only no. Do you understand my love?"

Then what I shall do now.

"You join me in the bathroom."

No, darling it would be too much. You take shower and come out then I shall go in bathroom. I am going for walk.

"In the rain you want to go for walk?"

I gone out in the portico and enjoyed rain.

I back in the bed and slept again.

She came out from bathroom. She prepared breakfast and tea. She was waiting for me to come and join breakfast.

"Where are you darling?"

I am in the bed my love.

"You get up and go in bathroom. Be quick otherwise I will not eat breakfast. I don't feel eating breakfast without you."

I brushed teeth, took shower and was ready for breakfast.

We ate breakfast after that she left for her flat to dress up and go for duty. She was in my kurta and payjama.

"I shall wake you up after reaching office. If you feel sleepy you can sleep."

That would be nice. At least I may get one hour sleep.

"Sure, I'll wake you up."

She kissed me and left my flat.

I got call from her and get ready for the office.

[9]

ONE EVENING WE WERE SITTING in the room. Rain started with heavy wind and storm. Coconut leaves, braches of trees, tin sheets of the roof were flying and falling on the ground. It was very awful. It was 8 o'clock, heavy rain continued and then all of sudden power failed. It was dark inside the flat and even outside also. She got scared and embraced me.

"Hold me tightly. I am scared. You heard sound of the wind. It is very awful."

I consoled her and asked her to leave me so that I can light a candle. In the light you will be fine and not scared.

"No. I won't leave you. You take me in lap and firmly hold in arms. Do not leave me alone. I fear very much in dark."

I am not going anywhere but in prayer room to bring candles and match box to light in the hall to get rid of darkness.

"I shall come with you holding your hand."

You come with me. Let us go in prayer room. Will you come behind me?

"No, I shall be with you holding your hand."

She put her one hand around my waist and I hold her in my arm. Slowly I manage to go with her in prayer room. She was stuck with door in prayer room and got little bit hurt.

I took candles and match box from table and lit the candle. Now there was light in the room. I took two more candles, light it and kept one in the hall and one in bath room.

"I am happy now. I was scared by darkness and thunder sound. Light give me relief. Now I am fine"

My flat was lit with candle light, bed room, hall and bathroom all. I drove away your enemy—darkness by lighting candles everywhere in the flat.

Now you can go anywhere in the flat without any fear. You can take few candles and keep them in your flat. So that you can use in case power goes off in your flat.

"I shall take some and keep them in my flat to use in situation like this."

I phoned Power Company to find out when power will be restored?

I got reply—It will take at least two more hours. A tree fell upon the power line and wire is broken. Emergency staff right on the job. Please bear with us.

Darling it will take three hours to restore the power. I think by that time we shall be late for dinner.

"Shall I warm food now if you are hungry."

Don't joke with me. How you will warm food when there is no power?

"I shall keep frying pan on stove and burn news paper and warm food."

Idea is not bad but I am not hungry at the moment. It is raining heavily, so let us enjoy drink.

"Yes, that would be fine. We can eat dinner after resumption of power."

Let me call my office to find out if any problem there.

"Do not call office. Why you are inviting problem yourself. If they have problem will call you."

Let us go for drink. She made two drinks and brought to me.

"Here is your drink. Cheers!!"

I said Cheers to her!

We sip drink. Good taste. You are perfect in making drink.

"You trained me. I must make perfect drink for my love."

Can you bring something to eat with drink? Just look in the chest drawers you will get salted peanuts and may be chips also.

She opened drawer and brought two packets one salted peanut and other potato chips.

"Here is two packets. Can you open them please?"

There is no plate where you are going to keep these.

"You open mean while I shall bring a plate. Do you need any things else."

No, Nothing just a plate.

"Here is plate."

I open packets and kept in the plate.

"Open your mouth and take few chips from my hand."

I took few chips in mouth from her hand. I also did same to her. She was sitting side by me and enjoying drink. She was cuddling in between also.

She asked me to open mouth for chips but took in her mouth instead mine.

"Kiss me—She asked me."

I kissed her on cheek, neck and then took her lip in mouth and suck like petal of orange.

She was much excited. Then I kissed her at neck and rubbed her breasts.

"I am getting excited. Please do something."

I stopped kissing and told her to finish drink first. We'll take one peg more, then dinner and go for bed.

She lay on my thigh face up looking in my eyes.

"Kiss me again on my lips as you did earlier."

I kissed her on lips. This time was stronger than earlier.

"You cut my lips. It is paining now."

I said sorry and gently rub her lips with my finger.

"Do not excite me more. Let me bring second drink."

She filled second peg for us. She asked to finish quick so that we take dinner. She was sipping drink hastily.

"You finish quick do not take too much time to finish drink. We'll take candle light dinner today."

I finished drink and we were on dining table eating dinner. We finished dinner and washed hands.

"We finished candle light dinner. Now let us have sex in the candle light."

We went in bed room to have candle light sex.

"You remove your clothes."

I was in night dress and I gave a dress to her. She kept it aside. She holds my dick and simulated. I was excited.

"She your dick is tight and hard. I want to have sex now. You remove your night gown otherwise I will tear it off."

She removed her clothes and was nude in front of me. She stripped me too. I asked her which pose she like to have sex today.

"I prefer the pose you did standing against wall beam and swing me forth and back."

Are you ready? I asked her.

"Yes, I am."

I took her near the beam on the wall and I stand against it. She hanged on my neck and I hold her from hips so that she climbed up at right position. I crossed my fingers and slide below her buttock. She was in relaxing state as her total weight was on my palms.

"I am ready now let me positioned cock against my pussy. Yes it is there. Please pull me little bit up."

I pulled her up.

"Yes it is ok and gone fully inside."

She put leg against wall and holds my neck and I gave her a swing.

"I am starting swinging now."

Ok swing. Oh..h.Oh..h she was crying and enjoying sex. She was fast.

"Kiss my tits and suck it."

I sucked her nipples little stronger.

"Ouch, you are doing hard please go easy."

I ease hold on her nipple and sucked gently.

"It is fine. I am nearing to finish please hold me."

I hold her so that she must get more pleasure.

"You make me spurt now. What about you? Will you continue or you also finished?"

I did not speak to her as I was at apex of sex and silently ejaculated inside her pussy.

I am exhausted—I told her after ejaculation.

I took her on the table as we were enjoying sex near it. I left her on table face up and went in bath room. She followed me quietly and cleaned mine before she cleaned her.

I was in kitchen. She came from back side and holds my waist. She started kissing my back, shoulder and neck.

I turned back and hold her in my arms, kissed her cheek and hold her cheek by my teeth.

"Ouch, you cut my cheek."

She went to wash room saw her face in the mirror.

"I got teeth mark on my cheek. You cut it. Someone will see then what she thinks about me. Even she may ask who cut it. It would be difficult to answer. You must gentle with me darling."

I said sorry to her and lifted her in my arms took on the table. She lay on table face up. I lifted her both the legs up on my shoulder and positioned my cock to her pussy and pushed in.

"Ouch! It is not at right position, painful. Take out, let me positioned it properly."

She holds my cock in her hand and set correctly.

"Push now—She asked me. Yes it is right. Go fast."

I was fast. She was enjoying.

"Yes there fuck me. Rub my breast also—she asked me"

I hold her both breasts in my hands and rubbed gently while fucking her fast.

"I ejaculated again."

Yes I am feeling that. It is much lubricated and something coming out too. I also ejaculated and then released her legs and slept over her. Lots of semen, discharge came out from her pussy. It fell on the table.

We rested in this position for few minutes mean while power resumed.

All the lights were on. We got up quickly and rush to bath room for cleaning and fresh up.

"What is next now?"

Warm milk and bring chocolate. Let us have some energy. She warmed milk and brought to me.

"Here is milk and chocolate for you."

We finished milk gone in the bed. Rain was continued. We slept holding each other whole the night. When we got up it was half pass five in the morning. We slept again because it was Saturday weekend for me and she has evening duty.

I got up at half pass eight. I asked her to get up and go for shower and fresh up.

"You go first I'll go later. I still feel sleepy my love."

You fresh up and take breakfast then sleep. It will be late and you may feel head—ache if do not eat breakfast and take tea.

"Then we both go together."

You must go first because you have to prepare breakfast for us.

"You prepare breakfast today."

I shall prepare breakfast today. You get up, go bathroom and fresh up.

"I know you won't allow me to sleep. I am going to fresh up."

She got up from bed and gone to bathroom. She peeps out through bathroom window—cool breeze and dazzling rain outside. She feels we should go out and enjoy this climate in the forest.

"Love outside is very pleasant. Let us prepare breakfast, go in the forest and had it there. We'll take shower in the dazzling rain. I hope you don't mind in accepting my proposal and fulfil my desire."

Let me see. I got up and gone in portico. Really it was pleasant outside—calm and cool breeze with dazzling rain. I accepted her proposal.

Right darling we shall cook breakfast and go out in jungle. Let me brush teeth.

"I am going wash room you brush your teeth outside. Then cook breakfast."

She was in bath room I brush my teeth and prepared two cups of tea for us.

"You may go bath room now. I'll take kitchen in my hand."

You prepare my favourite breakfast—Upma. I shall be quick. I went in bathroom, fresh up and back.

"Here is your cup of hot tea. Upma will be ready soon. What else you want to take there?"

You take plastic sheet, towel, shampoo, plates, pickles and spoon. Also take water and soft drink with you. If you like to take coffee then prepare it and fill in the thermos flask.

"I am collecting all these items while milk kept on stove for boiling to make coffee. Where is bag?"

Take from the storeroom. You select handy and water proof type.

She collected all the items in the bag and took disposable plastic bags for breakfast and soft drink. She took one bag for thermos flask.

"I am ready darling. You take car key and let us go out."

You are in night dress. Will you change it?

"I have kept good one inside the bag. I shall wear it after shower. I am wrapping towel around me while in the car."

We both started for enjoyment in the forest. It was not far from my flat just five kilo meters away. I reached in jungle and selected a lonely good site surrounded by trees and bushes.

"This is good place. Park your car under tree. See grass on the ground looks like green carpet."

I parked car under tree. It was not visible from the approach road. We came out of the car and enjoyed rain. We ate breakfast first under the tree in dazzling rain and then planned to have shower.

It started heavy rain again and visibility gone very low. You can't see trees fifteen meters away. I asked her let us go for shower. She was ready, took shampoo bottle and we both were enjoying shower under heavy rain. We were completely wet. Looks like coming out of pond. I removed my clothes but under wear.

"Apply shampoo on me all over my body. I am removing all my clothes."

I took bottle and applied shampoo on her head, body, and other parts of the body. I was rubbing her body and rubbed her breast. She got excited and took shampoo bottle from me.

"I am going to apply on you."

She put some on my head and then on my body. She stripped off me and applied on my genital area and on dick.

"Hey it was very small in size approx an inch and half before I applied shampoo. Now it is quite long approx eight inches or more. Marvellous I love it. It seems you are in urge of sex now."

Yes, I am in urge of sex. You touched mine and I got excited. Let us have sex now. I pulled her in my arm; under shower of heavy rain on green carpet of soft grass we had sex. It was vigorous sex. She enjoyed in standing and lay down poses. She was completely satisfied, exhausted and tired.

"Let us finish bath now. We had enough for today."

She started rubbing my back and gave tender touch on my head. Rain washed all shampoo from our head and body. We were clean and fresh.

"Let us go near car and get me towel so that I can change."

Just wait few minutes more rain is going to stop.

"No, I am shivering now and may get cold. Please give me towel."

I open dickey and took big umbrella—beach Umbrella from it. I took towel and called her under the umbrella.

"Aha!! You brought umbrella too. It is nice and quite big. I can change now."

You are nude what you want to change? You dry yourself with towel under umbrella and sit in the car and wear your dress.

"Yes you are right. I am coming under the umbrella you help me. Please dry me with towel."

I wipe her body with towel while she was holding umbrella.

"Let me wipe you please hold umbrella."

She wiped my body with towel. I dried my head and her head too.

We sit inside the car in dry clothes. Wet clothes were taken in the plastic bag and kept in the dickey of car. We took cup of coffee. She was resting on my arms and enjoying coffee. Now we felt warm and energetic. We were enjoying rain and had snap in the car. I asked her to give me another cup of coffee.

"Here is your cup of coffee. I am also taking mine cup."

You finish all coffee. Do not leave in the thermos. Now rain is slow down. We'll go home after coffee.

"I finished my cup what about you?"

I gave empty cup to her. She kept it in the plastic bag.

"I am ready now. Start your car and let us go home. What is time now?"

Time is twelve o'clock.

"It is half pass twelve. Let me cook lunch for us. I have to be ready for duty."

She asked me what to cook in the lunch. Purees and vegetable would be quick and go better with climate.

"All right, I am cutting vegetable you have to make purees."

Yes I am making purees you cook vegetable.

"I have cut vegetable and going to fry it now."

I mixed flour, water and kneaded well and it was ready for purees. I am rolling purees you please fry it now.

She kept frying pan on stove and poured oil in it. She heated oil.

"It is ready now. You have to be fast in making purees."

I rolled purees very quick. She fried all purees.

"We finished cooking. Lunch is ready. Let us go for it."

I think a peg of whisky will be good, if you make for us.

"I shall make drink of whisky for you only. I will take soft drink because going for duty."

As you wish. She gave my drink and took her soft drink. We were on dining table. She served lunch in the plate. I asked if she could take a sip from my glass.

"I will sip only once bring your glass."

I hold glass in my hand and she took a sip from it.

"Are you happy my love?—she asked me."

Yes I am happy darling.

She finished her drink and then lunch.

"I am going for coffee before start for work. Shall I make for you also?"

No, I shall sleep now. Give me a wake-up call at six in the evening.

"Time is quarter pass two now. I am going to dress up and get ready for work. I shall wake you up darling."

She took coffee and left for her flat.

[🜨]

WAS IN MARKET WHILE DOING some official work. I found special dresses on sale. I purchased two for her and one for me. There were special seven panties in a pack. Days were written on them. I asked shopkeeper if he has bra pack also for each day like panty. He smiled and said no, no such thing but I can give you seven different designs which you can use one a day. I purchased that also of her cup size.

I came back home and kept above items packed in the store room.

"I am inviting you at my home to night for dinner darling. She phoned me from work."

What's special? Are you celebrating some special occasion? We generally meet every day on either diner or lunch at my home.

"Yes something special to night."

Will you mind sharing me?

"I'll tell you but not now when we meet in the night then."

You are at work when you will finish your duty?

"I am in morning duty and will back at three or max half pass three in afternoon. There will be some of my staff from hospital. Party will start at eight in the evening."

It seems to be a big party. How many staff you are expecting? Do you need something I can arrange?

"No, nothing require from you today. Sisters, on their off today, are cooking dinner at my home. Drink will be arranged by Nutrition and cake by a local sister. It is homemade free of eggs. Everything is arranged you have to come in the party."

This is surprise for me. Can you tell me occasion so that I may come with suitable gift in the party?

"You will know when you come to my flat. I am hanging now will talk to you later."

I finished my duty at half pass four. I came home changed my dress and got ready for evening walk. Just as curiosity I gone to her flat to see what is going on. I heard from staff working in her flat about the occasion. It was her marriage anniversary. I completed my evening walk, rested and took shower. I took a cup of tea and packed what all I had purchased for her. It was a medium size packet. I dressed and took packet kept on the table. I was looking on clock. It was half pass seven only. When it will be eight, I was restless, roaming here and there in the flat. It was ten to eight when I left my flat for her. What they may say? Why I came early?

I was in her flat asked for Sandra.

One of the staff called her she someone has come to see you.

"Who has come? Where is he?"

I came forward and handed over the packet. Wish you happy anniversary. May God keep your married life pleasant and give all happiness in future life.

"Thank you for the nice gift."

Her eyes were full of tears. I wipe her tears with tissue paper. Do not spread pearls on the floor. You should happy today and always. She fell in my arms and thanked.

I hugged her and asked her to maintain party decorum because all are watching her.

She gone in side bed room and changed her dress which I bought for her. It was light blue in colour with pink flower print on it. She was looking more beautiful in this dress.

Party started at eight. Those invited has brought some gift for her, and wishes her marriage anniversary.

Drink was served to all of their choices. Sandra introduced me to all invitees in the party because I was only outsider all others were from hospital and well known to each other.

She introduced me to her hospital staff. She became emotional and said.

"He is all in one for me. I will never forget help and assistance he provided to me. I hope he will continue in future also. I salute him, I respect him and I love him."

All the staff applauded—ho ho ho!!!

One of the staff came forward and filled glass of the all in the party and requested us to stand up as Sandra is going to cut cake.

Cake was kept on central table all stand around it. Sandra took knife and blew off candle. She asked me join to cut the cake.

"Please come and help me in cutting cake."

I am not entitled for this work. Please excuse me.

"Then I shall not cut cake. Let party go as it is."

All in the party said please help her nothing will happen.

I join hand and cut the cake. All present sang the song for happy anniversary to Sandra. They took pictures of this moment also.

I took a piece of cake put in her mouth. She bites a little and rest I took. She did same to me.

Three cheers to Sandra on her anniversary. Hip hip hurray! Hip hip hurray!! Hip hip hurray!!!

Cake was served to all there followed by dinner. People enjoyed dinner. Staff cooked mouth watering food. I thanked to the staff those has cooked food.

Dissert was served after dinner and people started music and dance. I and Sandra danced on the floor. Slowly people were started going home.

Sandra was saying good night, thanks for coming to everyone.

I also requested Sandra for leaving to my flat.

"No you will not go unless every one leaves my place."

It was twelve in midnight few staffs were there and packing left over as take away. All the people left her flat by half pass twelve.

"See all the people left my flat, leaving us, husband and wife to enjoy. Now we shall enjoy married life. You are my husband. We cut the cake holding hands and you fed in my mouth. We have some pictures also which I will give you after it delivered to me."

Well that is fine. Why you became emotional in front of all the staff you fell in my arms. Do you think it was fine?

"I am yours. When I see you I am unable to control myself. Please forgive me for that.

I want one thing from you today please do not say no. I want to carry baby from you. He would be symbol for our love. When and how it is possible I will tell you later."

What happened to you today? You wanted such thing which is unbelievable. You are the same who do not want to carry baby from me earlier. Why you changed now?

"I want a good looking boy like you whom we'll give a good education to be either medico or technocrat."

We shall talk that later. It is too late in night. Shall I go now?

"Darling you must enjoy today whole night with me. This opportunity is yours. I shall not change the dress unless you enjoy removing these clothes. Come on now."

She pushed me in the bed and switched main light off. She switched on night lamp which spread light blue colour. She asked me to remove her clothes. I removed my paint shirt and kept aside. Later removed her clothes and left on the bed itself. Finally we were naked. She asked me to enjoy the way I like. We had sex in her flat.

"Why it is giving more pleasure today?"

You are happy and today your marriage anniversary that's why you are feeling more pleasure. Do you want to come up and enjoy.

"Yes, once you finish and will take rest then I'll come up."

I was enjoying much gentle touching her breasts, kissing her lips, pumping fast. She was feeling pleasure and some time crying too. I was on apex and ejaculated. She also discharged and all the discharge fell on the new dress kept on the bed.

I hold her in the arms and rested for some time.

"Let me go bathroom to clean. I shall back quick."

She cleaned her and called me to clean it. Later we back in the bed. She removed her dress from the bed and kept on the floor.

"Let me climb up on you. You lay in the bed face up. I want to enjoy much."

She sat on my thigh and holds my dick and put it in her pussy. Her hands were on my shoulders and she was pumping.

"Please rub my tits by your hands."

I rubbed her breast gently. It gave her more excitement and she was fast. I hold her shoulder and pulled her against my dick.

"Ah ah! It is fully in now, I am on fix can't move up and down. Can you please release you hold. Let me enjoy."

I soften my hold and asked her if it is ok.

"Yes, now it is fine. I am nearing to discharge."

Finally I pulled her from shoulder and dick was fully engaged in her pussy.

"Please lay me in bed I discharged now."

I lay her in the bed. I gave a towel to clean genital area. We hold each other and slept till morning.

"She got up at half past five and woke up me. Will you go for morning walk?"

I said yes. I dressed and came out for the morning walk. I went to my flat as it was little early. I saw my face full of lipstick marks. She kissed me in morning while wake up me. I fresh up cleaned face, took shower and prepare tea. She also came to my flat and joined on tea. I asked—Why you came to me?

"I forget to give you items for breakfast and some cake. You came quickly while I was in the bath room. So I thought I must give you and say thank you."

Thank you for the nice breakfast and cake. Now I need not prepare breakfast but a cup of tea.

"Shall I leave for my flat?"

As you wish. You can take rest here. What is your duty today?

"I am in night duty will leave at half past ten. I have to go my flat and clean what we have made dirty in the night."

You clean floor of the flat and bring cloth for washing in my flat.

"I will go later. Switch on Air condition I want to sleep now."

I switched on air con. She was in bed under blanket and slept.

I got ready, kissed her and started for work locking her inside my flat sleeping.

You have bought so many things for me on my anniversary while I have not informed you about this. How do you know about this? When you purchased gift for me?"

I was in the market when I saw seven days pack of the panty. I purchased one pack. I asked shopkeeper for matching bras of your cup size so he packed both. Blue colour dress is attracted me hence I asked him to pack that too. I have purchased all just a day before. I wanted to surprise you.

You have invited for dinner I came to your flat while going for evening walk and heard murmuring your friends about anniversary. On the way back home I purchased gift wrapper, packed all and gifted to you.

"I like blue colour very much. I open your gift packet and dressed in blue-red. How I was looking in that dress?"

You are beautiful and dress has added many folds in it. I would have lifted you but in the party girls were present. They might propagate it in other way. So I remain calm. You were looking like angle in the party.

"I was waiting party to over. All the girls left by one o'clock. I was sure they can stay up to one. I was little doubtful if some girl got drunk then she may stay till morning and may request for sex with you."

I would have left party long ago in such situations. I can't have sex with anyone.

"I would have asked her to leave the place as party is over in such situation. I do not share my love with anyone else."

95

You wanted to carry baby from me when you changed your mind?

"I have expressed my concern on this. We shall plan our leave together. Just before proceeding on leave we shall try for this. We'll not take any precaution for pregnancy. Fifteen days here or there does not matter in pregnancy to ascertain who is father of the baby.

During transit we shall stay in same hotel room. There will be good chance that we enjoy and try maximum to get pregnant. I know technique will use that at the time."

That sounds good. I shall try to fulfil your desires. If you have any other wish let me know.

"We are playing most of the day except my night duties that also two to three times which is quenching my sexual desire presently. You are taking care of me so much that my other desire fulfilled. You ask me my well being and taking care of food by cooking variety of dishes of my choice, delicious mouth watering. What else a woman wants? I request you to keep this going. You fulfilled my desire. Please do not stop."

Darling I shall try to fulfil all your desires within my hand. You don't worry.

"Can we go to market today?"

Yes we can. What do you want from market?

"I just want to roam and see what is available in supermarket."

Like what, food stuffs, fruits, drinks, clothing's, novelty items, etc etc.

"I want to see novelty items and drinks."

Fine, get ready we shall leave at half pass eight. By this time everyone back to their flat from the market. We can nicely see items enjoy evening on beach and back to flat by ten. Let us take dinner in the hotel today.

"Yes, it is ok for me. I am accepting your suggestions to pass evening on beach and take dinner in the hotel."

We started at half pass eight and reached supermarket. She was looking for clothing.

"I am looking for a nice light blue shirt. Please help me."

I asked shop keeper to show us light blue shirt. He brought two full sleeve blue shirts one was plain other was having thin design on it.

"Which shirt you like most?"

It depends upon for whom you are buying and what he likes. If you are asking my opinion then I prefer thin design on blue. It looks nice.

"Well then I am buying the shirt you said. It is appealing to me too."

For whom you are buying?

"I am buying this shirt for someone special to me. He is one among millions. He is kind hearted man. He is loving and caring person. He is almost like you."

Well, nice to know your choice and the man who cares you. Definitely he may be special man for you. Can we leave supermarket now?

"Yes, let me pay at counter and collect shirt."

I shall pay for you. Don't worry.

"No, not for this I shall pay for. I am having money."

She paid at counter and collected shirt. She kept it in the car and asked me to come to beach.

"Let us pass some time on beach. It is nice and cool."

We sat on the beach. She put her head in my laps and lay on the beach. She put her fingers on my head and then pulled me on her face. I kissed her and move my finger in her hairs, and then on lips. She took my finger in her mouth and sucked.

"I am excited now. Please do something here or took me home."

We started from the beach and reached a restaurant. I asked her what she wants to order in dinner.

"You know my choice is same as yours. I like food which you like. So please order the dinner I am hungry."

I ordered two beers and dinner two plates. Waiter brought two rose flowers, towels, spoon, fork and plates on the table. I gave a rose flower to my love. I wish you pleasant and happy evening.

"Thanks for the flower. May God keep you like this flower to spread smell all around?"

Waiter brought drink and roasted peanuts

We enjoyed drink and dinner in the open sky of the restaurant near beach in natural cool breeze.

"It is eleven in the night. Shall we go now?"

Yes darling we'll go home. Just wait for the bill. Waiter brought bill in the folder. I checked bill amount and kept 30 dollars in the folder.

I asked darling let us go now.

"How much bill was?"

It was twenty seven dollars. I gave three dollars tip to waiter.

"Then it is fine. You know here some restaurant do not like tips."

May be darling, we are not going restaurant more frequently. So I have no idea.

"Please hold me and take to the car. I feel drowsy."

I hold her and she put her hand around my waist and reached to car.

I open door asked her to sit then closed the door. I back in the driving seat, started car and came on the road.

She was excited much and put her hand on my dick by opening zip of the paint. I asked her—what you are doing. It is not good as I am driving.

"I can't wait now. I want to have sex. Drive fast please."

I reached home in fifteen minutes. I parked car and open door for her. I hold her and took in the flat.

You go bathroom change and come in the bed.

"Ok my love. I am going."

She changed and came in the bed. I also changed my dress, took blanket and came in the bed. I kissed her, rubbed her tits and sucked. She was excited much and stripped me off.

She stripped off herself. We enjoyed sex. It was little longer, some painful but over all joyful.

"I discharged now. What about you?"

You must have experienced mine. I also ejaculated.

"Let me come from bathroom. The drink made me drowsy."

It is effect of the cool breeze at beach. You get drunk even just in two cans of beer.

She was in bed. We were chit chatted for some time. She again excited and came on me. She took dick in her pussy and started enjoying. This time she stays longer and finally after seven minutes she discharged.

"Darling we had only two rounds. Still two rounds left."

Yes, we had finished two rounds—two were better and too strong. Let us sleep now rest leave for morning.

"That's fine. Good night then."

I kissed her and said good night.

As usual we hold each other experience hot breath from each other and slept.

One round we did early in the morning before starting day. She was happy but tired in the morning session.

"I shall sleep after you go to work. We shall meet again in lunch. I have evening duty today."

I went for morning walk and back after thirty minutes. Took little rest, fresh up and after prayer came on dining table. We both took breakfast—toast butter and glass of milk. I got ready for work. Hugged her, Kissed and started for work.

"Bye darling. Have a nice day."

Bye.

[12]

ONE DAY SHE WAS IN morning shift. She came at three and stayed in my flat. I came from work and saw her tired. What happen you look tired?

"I am having stomach pain today. I have not taken lunch at work. It is paining too much."

Why you have not consulted doctor at work? You must take some medicine. May be it is due to gastric? May be you have not taken lunch.

"I have taken medicine for gastric but of no use. I am going to sleep. Please do not disturb me."

All right, you take rest. I gave a glass on butter milk with pinch of powder of roasted cumin seed and black salt. It will help in soothing your pain if it is due to gastric problem. She took a glass and slept.

"I am little fine. I will not take dinner."

Why you will not take dinner? You will be all right by that time. Take one dose extra.

"I do not want take too much medicine. Can you give me hot water bottle? I will keep on stomach and get relief if gastric problem."

I gave her hot water bottle. I left for evening walk and back after forty five minutes. I have not gone longer as she was sick. I took rest without disturbing her sleep. I cooked light dinner vegetable briyani and lentil soup.

I took shower, performed prayer and prepared two cups of coffee. I woke her up and gave a cup of coffee.

"Thanks for the coffee. I got little relief in the pain but not complete. I will not take dinner."

Why you will not take dinner. I have cooked light dinner for us today.

"What you have cooked?"

I cooked briyani and lentil soup. Hope it would be fine and gentle to your stomach.

"If I skip dinner may be I get relief. Please do not force me for dinner today."

You have skipped lunch what happened. Do not sleep without eating dinner. Take as much as you feel comfortable. I'll not force you to take more. What duty you have tomorrow.

"I have morning duty tomorrow as well."

Fine, take dinner and get rest you will be fine by morning.

I served her dinner as much as she asked for. I asked if she is comfortable.

"Yes, I am full and happy. I hope there should not be stomach-ache."

I also hope so. Please come and take rest. I arranged bed for her. She wanted blanket because of air condition I gave to her.

She slept whole night and got up on alarm. She went in bathroom to fresh up. I prepared breakfast for her.

"I am not feeling hungry. Can I get only coffee please."

I gave her coffee and packed her breakfast and instructed to take upon reaching at work.

I asked her to get checked by gynaecologist.

"I am not in family way to get checked with gynaecologist. I will tell doctor that pain is still there. Medicine is not giving relief to me."

It would be fine. She consulted same doctor and he referred to gynaecologist for check up. Gynaecologist checked and took sample from her vagina. She did biopsy and gave sample for analysis.

She changed her medicine. With this medicine she got relief little bit. She was happy.

She came back and stayed in my flat. I came from office and found she was waiting for me with cup of tea.

"You suggested and doctor also referred me to gynaecologist. Dr. has given medicine which gave relief to me. I am fine now."

That is great news. Take complete medication and you will be all right again.

"I am going to take rest. You go for evening walk. You woke up me upon arrival from walk."

I back from evening walk, as usual took rest then shower and prayer. Later I went in kitchen make coffee for us. I woke her up. Darling coffee is ready.

"Give me my cup."

She sipped and commented.

"Coffee is nice thanks for this."

I am going to cook dinner you may take rest. I shall call you when it is ready.

"No, I am fine now. I also join you in cooking dinner."

I hold her and took to dining table. I gave carrot, cucumber and spring onion to cut for salad. I cooked lentil soup, rice and vegetable.

"I will take chapattis. I am not feeling eating rice."

I shall prepare quick give me few minutes.

"I am hungry now. Make quick please."

You serve dinner in the plate mean while chapattis will be ready. I started making chapattis.

I gave her chapattis and asked to start.

"I shall not take dinner alone. You come then."

I prepared all chapattis and joined her on dining table.

We finished dinner and ready to go in bed. Shall I give you milk?

"No, doctor has not allowed take milk and spicy food."

I also not taken milk and gone in the bed.

"I am fine now and want to have sex."

She was in night gown and removed that on the bed. She holds my dick, simulated.

No, you are sick. Take rest. Sex may be harmful in this situation.

"Come on let me have sex. Nothing will happen. I am fine now."

She climbed on me and took my dick in her pussy but cried. I asked her what happen.

"Why your dick is thick today. I am feeling its thickness has increased."

What you are talking just in few days you lived without sex and today you are telling it is thick. It is same as it was earlier darling.

"But I am feeling hard and thick."

Hard is fine as we are mating after a week but thick is ruled out. If you are feeling pain then do not do it.

"No, I am fine and let me enjoy. Do not disturb me. Simulate me by rubbing my tits and kissing me."

I rubbed her breast and kissed. She was pumping fast and discharged in few minutes. All discharge was on my genital as she gone off from the dick. I cleaned with soft towel. I asked her if she is fine.

"I am fine. Please you fuck me. Come on."

I fucked her. She cried in joy and then feels my ejaculation.

"Let us sleep now. We finished sexual session for today."

What duty you have tomorrow?

"I am again in morning. Whole week they gave me morning duties."

Ok then sleep now. You have to get up early in the morning. We slept holding each other.

Morning I prepared breakfast for us. She packed her and left for duty. I gone for walk, fresh up and performed prayer.

I finished my breakfast and started for duty.

In the evening I rang up her but could not get response. I check her flat but was locked. I was surprised where she might have gone.

Finally I rang hospital. Hospital informed me that she is admitted due to stomach pain. I started my car and reached hospital. I went in the ICU where she was admitted. I asked her about pain.

"I am still having pain. It was very severe in the morning after eating breakfast. I took medicine but pain was not subsidised. I called doctor and she has admitted me for some more tests. I shall be discharged after a day or two. I shall call you to pickup me."

I am coming back with dinner for you. I may stay here whole the night. May be you require some help.

"She laughed. You go home, take dinner and sleep well. I can't eat dinner from outside. Doctor has prescribed diet for me. Hospital will give me. In case I need help will call you darling."

I feel bad to take dinner alone. I do not know how I'll eat dinner alone. How I will sleep alone. Can I come and sleep here?

"No, you have to change your habit now. You go home without fear for me. You should attend your duties. If you sleep here girls will tease me. They will ask—Is he your boy friend. You will be known to all in the hospital as my boy friend. I hope you will take care of all these."

I also supported her and left hospital after kissing her. I came home and fresh up. Cooked dinner, took a can of beer, say cheer for her health. I started dinner but don't feel eating. I took some and rest I kept in the fridge.

I warmed milk, took it and gone in bed. I was trying to sleep but could not. I don't know when I slept but got up after alarm buzzed. I skip morning walk got ready, took my breakfast and started for hospital. I reached hospital but she was not in ICU. Hospital staff informed me that she is taken for ultrasound after that she will go for x-ray. You can't meet her in the morning but afternoon.

I waited there for one hour and then started for duty. I was feeling uneasy on that day. Staff asked me if something wrong with me. I said nothing but could not sleep properly in the night. I attended few call duties and then left for home.

In the lunch I prepared lunch and then called hospital enquired about Sandra. Staff on duty told me she is sleeping as anaesthesia was administered her during test. I was wondering what are tests has been conducted on her.

I took lunch and slept for one hour. I reached late for duty. After my duty I went hospital to see her.

"Hi, I am sick now. So many tests conducted on me. Blood and flesh sample taken for examination. We shall get result in a week."

I saw weakness on her face. She was hopeless too. I tried to console her but being medico she knew much better on the case. I boldly said about will power. If your will power strong you can fight any disease and get rid of. If your will power is weak you can't fight,

She was aware I am God fearing and what say is correct. She smiled and whispered—

"That's why I surrendered to you. I trust in you."

Doctor's report says that one day more she will be observed and then discharged. I was with her for two hours and talking about her health.

"I am worry about my kids. She said in tearful eyes."

God is great. Why you are thinking so much. You will get rid of this disease. You will be back in your kids.

"You go now it is time for serving dinner. Sisters may object and complain to doctor on duty."

I kissed her and started my car for home. I got fresh up and cooked dinner. A friend of mine visited me and asked about sadness on my face. I lie to him telling having headache. He left me then I took dinner and gone on bed.

In the morning I visited her before going to work. She was cheerful and told me she was waiting for me.

"I know you will come before going to work. I may be discharged today."

That's great news. I went to work but there was nothing much to do. Everything was normal.

I called her in hospital asked about reports.

"All reports are normal awaiting only flesh report which has been sent to overseas for test. Hopefully I shall be discharged today in the evening."

I back home, cleaned all the rooms and vacuumed hall carpet.

In the evening I gone to hospital from work but learned she was discharged at three o'clock and dropped at her place.

I came home and found she was not there. I went to her flat girls were murmuring with her.

I back to my flat and rang as per code. She has not responded to my phone. I was in tension why she is not lifting phone.

I went for evening walk and then cooked dinner. I took beer and was enjoying. I tried her phone again but was busy. Finally I got her response. I asked why she not lifted my phone.

"All the girls were around me and you were ringing. I know it was you so I kept ringer off. Girl left me at half pass six. Since then I was trying you but not getting answer from you. I realized you may be on evening walk. Just few minutes back I tried you but phone was busy. To whom you were talking?"

I was trying you and getting your number busy. I think we were trying each other and getting number busy.

"Just now I got you. What are you doing?"

I cooked dinner and taking beer. I am talking to you now. Let me know your program.

"I want you come to my flat with dinner. I am tired and feel sleepy but hungry too."

I am coming give me few minutes. I packed dinner and dressed up left for her flat. I reached her flat and pressed door bell. She open door for me. I kept dinner on table and hugged her.

"My darling I am fine now. Pray God nothing come in the flesh test which was taken by biopsy."

I always pray God for your well being. Hope that test also will clear you from all the disease. I guess you have only gastric problem. It will be cured.

"Please serve dinner. I am hungry."

I served dinner in the plate:—Rice, bread, vegetable and lentil soup. I asked her to say grace and then took dinner.

"I was fed up with food served in the hospital. It was really test less but what to do doctor has not allowed take food from outside. I am taking today delicious dinner."

It's ok darling. You sleep now I go to my flat. We shall meet you tomorrow. What duty you have tomorrow.

"Doctor has given me bed rest for a week. I shall not go to work for one week."

Fine then take rest I will bring breakfast in the morning and meet in the lunch.

"Darling it is ok. Please hug me once more."

I hugged her, kissed and left her alone in her flat. I asked to keep her phone normal and call me if she needs any help in the night.

"O.k. darling I shall call you if require help from you."

Bye bye for now. I left her flat.

I came back in the flat and warmed glass milk which I take after diner. I arranged bed and slept after finishing milk.

I was in sound sleep. I got phone call from office. I rush to office to check the problem and fixed it. I back at two in the morning and slept. I got up at six. Prepared breakfast fresh up and took breakfast parcel for her. I deliver breakfast in her flat. Kissed her and gone to work.

I back from office in the lunch and found she was in my flat. She cooked lentil soup and rice in lunch. Why you have taken pain for cooking lunch? You must take rest.

"I have prepared lunch without any strain on me. I have not baked bread standing for longer time at cooking range. I left that for you."

Fine I will bake bread for us. I changed and started making bread. It was ready in few minutes. We took lunch together and then little rest before going to office.

"Here is your cup of coffee. Fresh up and get ready for work."

I fresh up took coffee and got ready for work. I kissed and hugged her before leaving for office.

"See you darling in the evening. I'll take rest here."

It would be fine.

Five days passed she was on rest. She was called for follow up by her doctor. She was checked and found normal. She was advised to take care in food. Do not take spicy food.

"Have you got report doctor?"

No, still not but may be get it in next week.

"Thank you Doctor. My medicine will continue or any change."

You will continue one more week same medicine. Hope you will cure soon.

"What about my duty doctor?"

You are fine now you must resume your duties. I'll give you fitness certificate. You give to admin.

"Doctor issued fitness certificate. I handed over certificate to admin and my duties were arranged."

She told me over phone she is fit for duty now. I was happy for her. Thanks God she back to work again.

What duty you have tomorrow?

"I am in the morning."

Well then we can meet in the evening in the dinner.

"Yes, we shall."

I back from work in the evening and then met her.

I was cooking dinner. She asked me to put small amount of spice and no chilly.

I cooked dinner without chilly. Dinner was ready. I called her for dinner.

"I am coming washing my hand."

She joined on dining table for dinner.

I asked her to serve dinner. She served dinner in the plates.

"You will say grace today."

I said grace and started dinner.

"It is delicious even without chilly darling."

Yes, it is. I have not added chilly for you. Your health is at first for me rather than taste. I can take green chilly if I need.

Once you declared free from disease and allowed to take normal food then we shall cook spicy food.

"Thanks darling for giving me support and taking care of me. I think without you I am meaningless."

We finished dinner and took glass of milk. I asked her where she will sleep.

"I shall sleep here with you."

She switched off light and we gone on the bed.

"Get me your dick while she stripped off herself."

Unless you completely fit you should not do this.

"I am fit, healthy and energetic. I can fuck you. So please help me in fucking. I am having this after a week."

Sickness will grip if you are not healthy. So better avoid it some more time.

"Please help me I beg you. Please get ready and come in the bed."

I changed my dress, gone in the bed. She makes me naked. She holds my dick and took it in her pussy and started fucking.

"Please hold me, rub my breasts and kiss tits."

I did all for her. She was excited much and started fast and cried out.

"Why it is thick now? What you did? Its thickness is increased. I feel it."

I have not done anything you are sick may be due to that you are feeling so. May be still you have some problem.

"I think doctor did biopsy. This could be one reason I am feeling so."

It means internal sore may be still there. You should not have sex in such condition.

"I feel so. May be you are right sore still there due to biopsy sample. I shall asked doctor and tell about this."

Fine let us sleep now. Morning we have to go for work.

"You please have sex with me again. Your dick is still strong and tight. You have not ejaculated."

No, let me like this and go for sleep.

"I want you to get enjoyment with me. Your help I can't ignore. You enjoy I am all right."

I fucked her hard. She was happy and enjoyed second time. We both discharged and her pussy was full.

"Please hold me and take to bathroom."

I hold and took her in the bathroom. She urinated and cleaned her pussy.

"Can I get toilet paper to clean vagina properly."

I gave her tissue paper and she cleaned. I also cleaned mine. I hold her and took in the bed and slept.

Morning we got up on time. Prepared breakfast, coffee and ready for work after eating.

"We shall meet in the evening darling."

She kissed me and gone to her flat to dress up for duty. I assured her and said bye.

She left early at six while I left at half pass seven.

She was on duty after a week. How she will be managing today being quite weak. I was assuming all these while I was on the work. Shall I call her? Then I realized I must not call her. She may be or may not pick phone. May be other staff attend the call.

Though we are going to meet in the evening so why should do this. Finally I decided will attempt from home during lunch.

I reached home in lunch break. Telephone was ringing. I lifted said hello!

"It is me darling. I am fine and doing duty. Stomach pain is very less but not completely gone. Hope I need more medication."

Well you are now under good doctor. She will take care of you. Keep informing her about your health. Also, take medicine as prescribed by doctor.

"Sure I shall follow her instruction and take regular medicines. I want to be fit as soon as possible. Today doctor has prescribed vitamins along with other medicine."

That is fine. You will be cured fast and health will improve. Your vitality will be maintained with vitamins. Shall I take lunch now?

"I am sorry, please go ahead and take lunch. I was free so talking to you so much."

It is all right. Now I shall take lunch and rest. We are meeting in the evening.

"Yes, we are."

I hanged phone. I took lunch in the plate, warm it in microwave and sit on dining table for lunch. I ate lunch and then took little rest. I went for duty after quarter pass one. I was busy at work and forgotten time. It was five, I started for home. I reached half hour late. I entered in the flat and found toast and tea on the table. She was waiting for me.

"Why you are late today?"

There was much work in the office. I finished by the time it was five. So became late today.

"Let us take snacks and tea."

You are also not taken any thing. You must take something every two to three hours to avoid gas formation.

"I have taken biscuit and then prepared snacks for us. I wanted to call you but thought you are on way. That is reason why I did not call you."

Yes, darling. Let me fresh up and then I will join you.

"I am waiting you come quick darling."

Fine, I am coming in few minutes. I changed and fresh up then join her on snacks. We ate snacks and then took rest. I asked her about report of biopsy.

"We are still waiting for the test result. Hopefully it will be available in this week."

I pray God the test result should be fine. You will be free from all the disease.

"I hope your prayer will be heard by God."

Are you going to your flat?

"No, I am staying here in your flat. Do you have any problem?"

No darling I was asking you. We shall then take rest.

"It is good to take rest some time. I shall get your company today."

We switched on radio and enjoyed music. While music was on I took a snap. She noticed me sleeping.

"You were sleeping during music on radio. I switched off so that your sleep may not disturb but you woke up."

It is fine. Now I shall take shower and perform prayer. We have to cook dinner.

"I shall make coffee for us."

Please start making coffee. I shall be quick. I took shower and then performed prayer while she was making coffee.

"Coffee is ready darling."

I am coming honey.

We enjoyed coffee. We sit in the portico while rain started. It was drizzling but enjoyable. We were there for thirty minutes.

"Let us cook dinner. I have morning duty."

I started cooking dinner. She helped me from outside. Dinner was ready in one hour.

"I shall serve dinner you come on the table."

We enjoyed dinner slowly. She was cheerful and happy. After a week she was taking spicy dinner.

"Let me take my medicine."

I gave her medicine bag. She took the tablets and capsules prescribed for evening dose.

"Give me a glass of water."

I gave her water. She took medicine.

"Let us go in the bed and sleep now. It is ten thirty now."

Yes darling let us go on the bed. We slept nicely without disturbing. She wake up at four and wake me up also.

"I want to have sex now. Please come on."

You are sick sleep now we shall have that later.

"No, I want now."

As you wish. We had sex. She cried again.

"I feel day by day your dick is getting thick and long."

No it is not. It is same as it was earlier.

"Why I am feeling so?"

You may be having wound inside which still not cured properly. You should tell doctor.

"What shall I tell? When I have sex I feel dick of my boy friend thick and long?"

I am sorry, you can't say that. But you can say that I am feeling pain inside my vagina. She will give some cream to apply.

"That is nice idea. I can tell this to doctor. Let me enjoy now. I will climb on you and enjoy."

She sits on my thigh and took dick inside and started enjoying sex. In few minutes she discharged and I also ejaculated. She took towel and cleaned genital area of ours.

"Now you hold me and enjoy."

I hold her is arms and enjoyed rubbing her breasts and sucked tits. Finally we excited again and had another round of sex.

"Now I am tired. Let us sleep."

We slept till morning and got up after alarm buzzed. We rush for fresh up. Took tea and she left for her flat to get dressed, go for work.

I went for morning walk and then fresh up, took breakfast and gone to work. It was very hectic day at work. Lots of complaints have to attend. I was quite busy at work could not call her. She also not called me. It was one o'clock in after noon I went for lunch in a Chinese restaurant. I back again at work. She called me in the office.

"I rang your home number at half pass twelve and office also but no response from you. Are you all right?"

I am all right. I was busy at work and could not go home in lunch. I took lunch outside today and come for work. How are you?

"I am fine. I shall talk to you in detail in the evening about my further follow up."

Take care will meet in the evening then.

"Are you quite busy today?"

Yes, I am quite busy. I have to attend lots of complaint in the afternoon session.

"Then I shall leave you. Come home soon. I shall wait you on tea."

Bye will meet you in the evening at tea.

We met at tea in the evening. What doctor said to you?—I asked her.

"Doctor called me tomorrow empty stomach. She will do some more check up and test to ascertain the problem."

It means you will go without breakfast. What she said about vaginal pain and your feeling about thickness.

"She will do check up tomorrow morning then she will tell me about this."

I pray God everything to be normal. You will get well soon.

"I am fine now. I need delicious dinner today."

What do you like to take in dinner?

"I like green Pease potatoes spicy vegetable, breads, rice and papad. I want ice cream after dinner."

You want to skip milk today.

"Yes, it will create gastric problem to me. I do not want to get stomach pain again."

As you wish. I started cooking dinner of her choice and it was ready by half pass eight. I told her dinner is ready when she likes to take.

"I think by nine it would be fine."

We switched on radio, listen some nice songs and by nine we started dinner.

"It is delicious as I desired. Thanks for the nice dinner."

No thanks. We should not say thanks to each other my love.

"Sorry for this."

Sorry also not to be said. We are friends and in friendship no sorry and no thanks please.

"Yes, my love. I am not only friend but your spiritual wife too."

We laughed—ha ha ha!!.

Let us sleep now.

"I will make bed you come later."

I went in when she called me. She was nude in the bed.

"Remove your clothes and then come in the bed like me."

You will be examined tomorrow morning. So avoid sex tonight. We'll enjoy next night.

"There is nothing to do with sex and stomach pain."

What about vaginal examination?

"She will do that. Nothing to worry, come on and enjoy with me."

We had sex. She was enjoying and crying too. I asked why she is crying.

"Nothing to worry, I am crying in joy. Your dick is gone too deep and giving a peculiar joy. I am feeling to cry due to pain but enjoying."

We had two round of sex in that night before twelve. Then we slept holding each other.

"Do not press my breast and pinch the tits. I shall get excited again. Then we do sex whole the night."

I stopped doing that and hold her in arms kissed on her on lips. We slept till morning.

She got fresh up and gone for duty. I was in morning walk and then fresh up. I took breakfast then gone for duty.

Doctor checked up her again. She found lump in the ovary at beginning. Doctor informed her that due to lump in the path of ovary you are feeling pain. We have to remove the ovary. You will be admitted in the hospital and in the afternoon I shall operate and remove ovary. She was much scared when heard the removal of her ovary. She called me in the hospital and informed about this.

I told her nothing to worry. It is a minor operation and would be recovered soon. She was crying and wanted opinion of her husband. I arranged call for her with her husband.

"I am having pain in the stomach. Doctor want to remove my ovary as a lump is developed at mouth of ovary. Shall I get operated here—she asked her husband."

Her husband asked her to come back to country and treatment will be made available to her. She should not get operated there. If something unusual takes place who will be responsible.

Doctor came back from lunch and started preparation for the operation.

"Doctor I talk to my husband. He is asking me to come back and get treatment there. So please discharge me I'll go to my country."

You know better it is minor operation. You will get cure within the week. You are a nurse you should consider your health. You might have seen so many operations I have done here like this.

"Doctor my husband wants me to come back. Please propose my departure."

Biopsy report was available to Chief Medical Officer (CMO). He informed the office to send her back to her country as she diagnose of deadly disease. He was in the process of the arranging her departure by next morning flight.

Doctor met Chief Medical officer in her case as she refused operation. CMO told doctor about report and about her departure. CMO asked doctor not to tell patient about disease.

She called me again in the office at four in the evening.

"Can you arrange air ticket for me?"

Yes I can. When you want to go?

"I want to go as soon as possible. Can I get tomorrow morning flight?"

I'll ask CMO if possible then I book for you. I am going to book for tomorrow morning tentatively. If approved I'll buy ticket.

"Fine you please ask CMO and arrange my ticket."

I went to CMO office but he was already left office.

I informed her about this and left her in the hospital.

"You come to me after booking air ticket."

I went airline booking office and booked a ticket for her. I told agent that ticket will be collected in the morning. Agent gave me PNR, reservation details printout. I came back to her in the hospital and gave her news that air ticket was booked for day after tomorrow. Her eyes were tearful. I can see that. It was neither of joy nor of sorrow but was on separation. I console her not to worry. Get well and back soon.

"I know that but I can't say how much time it will take may be a month or more. May I be permitted by my husband to come back or not? I will never ever forget you and help you extended for me."

A Sister came and asked her to go home. You are discharged from hospital.

"All right, I will change and back. You just wait here."

She changed her dress and took medicines. She came with me to my flat.

"I am happy that whatever time I have, will stay with you."

I welcome her stay. We took a cup of coffee. We took rest after that. I was tired due to much work in the office and visiting hospital. I slept. She was on chair near bed. She was desperately thinking about her sickness. She tried to pull blanket over me and her tears fell on my face. I woke up and asked her why she is weeping.

She clung on me and started weeping. I hold her in my arms and console her that I will phone her every day till her back again.

"Promise you will ring every day."

I promised darling. Now you stop tears.

"Can I cook dinner today?"

Yes why not. You can cook whatever you like.

"I like simple vegetable briyani and lentil soup."

Go ahead in kitchen. I shall fresh up and join you after prayer.

"Pray for me to get cure soon."

Of course darling, I shall pray for your wellbeing. I went in bathroom and took shower, performed prayer and come back in the kitchen.

"Briyani is ready cooking soup now. It would be ready in few minutes. Can I get a beer today?"

Yes darling you can take a can of beer. I am also taking beer. After taking beer we took dinner and then gone in the bed.

"I will be cure and then back again darling. Take care of my flat in my absence. I'll give your name officially"

Sure darling I will see your flat everyday and sit there few minutes to see your clothes and assume that you are still with me.

"You love me too much. Darling you take care of yourself and keep in touch."

Sure darling. Now let us sleep.

"Yes we should sleep. You have to go morning duty."

Let us sleep. You are also tired today. What examination doctor did today?

"She put her hand in my ovary and looks for problem. She found a lump in the opening of ovary. Further you know she wanted to operate it."

It was painful examination. Now you take rest and sleep well.

"I want to have sex before go for sleep."

I think we should not go for sex. It would better for both of us.

"Nothing to worry, I can't sleep without sex darling. Help me few days more. I don't know when we shall meet again."

We had sex. She was up and enjoying. It was painful for her but enjoyment to her satisfaction.

"Please drop semen in side. Do not feel insecure. It will be fine for me."

I ejaculated inside her and she also discharge. She kept holding me after ejaculation in the same position.

Why you not allowed me to take out?

"I want to enjoy much. So I hold you. Warm fluid inside pussy gives different feeling. I wanted to enjoy that moment."

After few minutes we disengaged and she cleaned her pussy with soft towel and slept.

We got up in the morning. I left for work after eating my breakfast. She remained in the flat.

"I got menstruation in afternoon. Please bring napkins for me."

In the evening I came back and gave her napkins. She was asking for air ticked. I told her that will bring in the morning.

In fact her air ticket was cancelled. I asked CMO office they informed me that administration is looking into it. She will get her ticket and other necessary assistance from office. You should not worry about her.

I was sad with this news and could not hide from her. My face was telling my unhappiness.

"Usually you were eager when come to home and stay with me. Why you are sad today?"

I am not sad just tired of work.

"You can't hide your sadness to me. I am with you almost a year. I know you better. Definitely there is something you are hiding to me."

Darling you should not say like this. I am not hiding anything to you. You will get ticket in the morning. I promise you. If office is not ready to give you I shall buy it for you.

"I know that darling. If you are happy then I'll get cured and recovered quickly."

I kissed her and my eyes were tearful. I became emotional told her how I shall stay without her.

"I shall get recovered and back soon even if I have to come against the wish of my family."

I was not able to console myself. Just she blackmailed me for her sexual requirement.

As usual we passed evening and time was for dinner. We took diner and then slept. This night I could not sleep well.

Whole the night I was thinking about her health and chances of recovery.

We got up in the morning. I kissed her and asked about her pain.

"I have less pain but she my stomach is swelling like pregnant women."

I saw and touched her stomach. It was soft but swollen like balloon. I asked her to contact doctor and tell her about your problem.

"I shall call her home after seven thirty. She may be sleeping. Her duty starts from eight thirty."

I did my usual routine and then fresh up got ready for work.

I was at work and looking for stuff she required to pack her personal thing. She got call from CMO office that admin staff is coming to pick her up and drop at air port. She is going home today. Flight will leave at eleven thirty. You get ready for this.

She tried me in the office but could not get me. She rang a friend of mine and told him that she trying for me but unable to get. Can you ask him to come back home urgently?

He came to my office but I was not in office. He was in search of me while we met in hospital. He informed me that Sandra wants you at home urgently.

I rush to home but she was not there. I gone to her flat she was there taking her personal belongings. Driver from hospital was there to drop her to air port. We packed her suitcase. I asked her to keep hand bag as light as possible.

Driver took her bag and suit cases in the car and asked her to come. She was in her flat wanted to kiss me—last kiss of the journey but could not as driver was present.

I took her flat's keys and told her that I am coming to air port.

"I shall wait you at airport."

I followed her but as per instructions driver took her directly in checked in passenger lounge. I parked my car and looking for her. Police allowed me to go in and met her.

I asked her air ticket and noted timing when she will reach Australia and when she will reach her home country.

I gave her ticket back. Told that—I shall be in touch with her.

"Ok darling I am leaving now. Only one **Kasak** is left. It will remain whole of my life."

Our eyes were tearful. We said good bye to each other.

"Bye bye."

I came out to see her while boarding in the plane and departure of the air craft. I found lots of the people assembled on first floor open area to say good bye to their loved one. I was also one of them.

I saw her boarding in plane climbing via stair case attached to plane. She was looking at me. I also waved my hand to say bye—bye to her. She waved her hand and entered in the plane.

Plane was full. All passengers boarded, checking was completed by ground staff then door closed. Now you can't see any one inside the plane. People assembled at the departure lounge at visitor gallery were left except me.

Plane left and all other people also left the airport but I was still sitting there and lost in her memories. One of the Air port staff came to me and said to go out let me close the door now.

I came down and then started my car reached home and took a glass of water.

I was not feeling to take lunch so just took a cup of tea and shed tears for few minutes and then someone buzzed my door bell. I kept cup in the wash basin and cleaned my face open door. He was my friend. He wanted to get lift from me to go his office as his car had flat tyre.

We started for work and dropped him to his office. I attended my office but did not carry out any work. I left office early for home. I told director that I am not feeling well.

I reached home. I took snacks and slept for one hour. I called her hotel in Melbourne. Unfortunately the phone was not working in the hotel room. I shouted on the hotel staff then Manager of the hotel promised me that telephone will be fixed within fifteen minutes.

I called her again after thirty minutes and got connected. I asked her well being. She told me that she was accompanied by two assistants from hospital to help her. They will assist her in Melbourne to get board in the plane for home country.

Are you fine? How is your pain? I asked her.

"I am fine with pain but stomach is swelling more."

You can asked air hostage to make suitable arrangement for you so that you can go sleeping in the plane.

"O.k. dear, I will ask them. Have you taken your dinner?"

Without you what dinner. I have not taken lunch even.

"You are doing injustice. Why you have not taken dinner?"

I was searching you. My heart was with you. I left airport at one, thirty minutes after flight took off. When reached at home started weeping as I am missing you. Somehow I could make a cup of tea and went for duty.

"You promised me that you will take care of yourself in my absence. If you are not doing that how do you think I'll get cured?"

I promised her that I will take care of mine as I was taking earlier. Have you taken some thing? What time hotel will serve you dinner?

"Yes I have ordered soup and dinner they will serve in fifteen minutes."

I shall call you in the night. I am going to cook dinner for me.

"You call me in the morning. I shall sleep because I am tired and swelling of the stomach makes me uneasy."

As you wish. Have a nice sleep. Good night.

"Thank you and good night darling!"

[13]

I CALLED HER IN THE MORNING. She was getting ready for airport. I talk to her. She was having swelling in the stomach and little pain also.

"I shall be leaving for airport in ten minutes. My bags are taken by assistant and they may be coming to take me to air port."

Fine, Then I shall call you tomorrow morning at home number. I will inform your home that you are reaching. Shall I ask them to come to airport?

"Yes, please. Though consul will be there but if my husband be present will be nice."

Don't worry I will ask him to reach air port at correct time.

"So nice of you,"

You take care. Bye.

"Have a nice day darling."

I went for work. I was feeling uneasy but when back from work I sat for prayer. I asked God to give me courage. She came to me for her requirement and as you suggested I help her. Now give me courage for passing time in my own self.

I started my normal routine and went for evening walk, took rest and then shower. I cooked dinner after performing prayer. I sit alone on dining table and took dinner.

I called her home and informed her husband that Sandra is reaching at midnight. I gave flight details and asked him to go airport to receive her.

I have gone in the bed after taking milk. I slept. I got up on alarm and started my routine.

I back in the lunch and took lunch then called her at home. I talk to her. Have you reached safely?

"Yes I reached and my husband was at air port to receive me."

Fine now you get checked with good doctor and take necessary medication to get rid of the disease.

"My husband has taken appointment with doctor and today evening he will take me there."

Ask your husband to give me telephone number of the hospital so that I may call you.

"I shall ask him. He will on pass telephone number to you."

Then I may be able to talk to you in the hospital.

"Sure, it would be great pleasure for me talking to you."

Bye for now.

"Bye."

I went to office and attended my duty. I tried to forget what has happen had happened. I must live life lovely.

I was able to re-collect all good things and tried to erase bad things from the mind. I use to sit longer on meditation. I do get courage to fight bad things in daily life.

Next day I called her husband and he gave telephone number of the hospital where Sandra was admitted. I rang Hospital and requested to connect Sandra. Operator extended telephone to her. I talk to her.

"I did mistake coming here. Doctors will examine and do all pathological tests and then operate to me. I am feeling more pain. My stomach is swelled and looks like having complete baby and will deliver soon. It is very pain full. I am crying but no one listening."

What can I do from here? Now you are with doctor in the hospital. They will take care of you.

"Please call me tomorrow also."

Sure I will call you to know your wellbeing. You will be all right and get well soon.

I called her next day but operator told me she is in the operation theatre. You call her tomorrow.

I was very sad as could not talk to her.

I called next day and came to know she was operated and doing well. Her operation was successful and she is recovering now. I was able to talk to her.

"I operated yesterday. Now swelling has gone and pain is also less. I have been advised to take chemotherapy after this. Hopefully within a week I shall be discharged."

Thanks God! You are safe and operation is successful. I pray God for your quick recovery. Take care and get well soon. Bye for now.

"Bye"

I was happy as operation completed without any complication. She was happy being with her children. She was nursing in the hospital for about fifteen days then discharged. I talk to her at home.

"I am in the home with my kids. My lovely hairs are falling now. I asked doctor about my hair loss. As per him, it is due to chemotherapy. Doctor said to me hair will grow again. I am fear of to become baldy."

Take all the medicine as prescribed by doctor. You must be careful in follow up. Do not miss any appointment with doctor.

"How are you? How things are there? Is anyone asking about me?"

I am normal now. Things are same as you have seen nothing changed. Hospital staff asked me about your wellbeing. They are sympathetic to you as you extended all possible help to them. Here if anyone is not happy that is me. I missed you in my daily routine. You should not be emotional and speak out something unusual.

"I realise that but can't do anything from here. I am writing you in details. Thanks for calling me. Bye for now."

It would be fine. Thanks and bye.

I received a letter one day. It was written by Sandra. She has written her feelings in this letter. I read the letter many times in many days and each day I found different meaning and feeling of her. I finally decided to keep this letter and read it when I met her.

I am writing few lines of her letter here.

"I could not accomplish my desire due to my sickness but still I have not left hope. Once I back after treatment will make it true. Please pray God for my quick recovery . . . !"

She further added—"I had done something unusual due to my strong desire which I desperately needed. What I have done to you when I think I hate myself. But what you did for me is unforgettable. I am thankful to you for accompany and fulfil my desires."

I used to go in the forest and sit under tree thinking of her. I get socked when remembering her words:-

"If my desire is not fulfilled you may be questioned in Police station. You do not have enough time to think. Tell me yes or No? Choice is yours."

I got frightened remembering above words of her. I later realized her strong desires and her feeling. Any one in that situation would have freely accepted and enjoyed that moment but I was not able to accept at all.

"If my desire is not fulfilled you may be questioned in Police station. You do not have enough time to think. Tell me yes or No? Choice is yours."

Finally what happened I was not responsible for that? I had lot more responsibility back at home. I do not want to be defamed in my own community. It was not easy to get a job in the age of near forty.

I had no option but to silently get raped, raped and raped. I was not in position to say anyone what happened to me and what is happening?

We used to communicate over phone. I enquired about her health.

"I am getting better but all my hairs are falling. Doctor is telling it is due to chemo therapy and will grow again. What about my job there?"

I told her that I have been called by administration to vacate your flat and keep all your personal belonging in my flat.

"It seems they are not going to call me back."

I shall enquire today about that.

"Fine let me know so that I may look for job here."

I shall inform you as soon as I get some news on this.

"That would be great help for me."

I enquired in her office and got report for her final payments. I checked the statement and found some mistake which I pointed out to the office and got corrected. I have been asked to give crate dimension for her person effects to be mobilized to her country.

I informed her about this. She was broke out due to this sad news.

"If I knew that I will not be call me back. I would have got operated there and have got free medical treatments. I did mistake, now I realised."

You are right. You became emotional at that time and decided to go back home for operation.

"I had suffered lots of pain during testing period before operation. I spend a lot on medical. I am having no savings. Now I lost my job also."

I conveyed here total amount which she will get and all her personal effect will be send to her. I asked her shipping address where she wants her personal effects to be delivered.

"You know my address on which you write letters. You send my personal effects on that address. I have no any dutiable items, so no problem with customs."

You have television set that is not duty free.

"I shall manage for that."

We finished our talk and hanged telephone.

I manage to get crates and packed her personal effects properly and handed over to admin for sending to her. The money received on her account was send to her native bank account which I gave to administration.

I informed her that money was send to her and her personal effect also.

"I will inform you once I receive it."

Bye for now.

"Bye."

I received call after fifteen days that she received her personal effects.

"I got all the items and TV set perfectly in good condition. Thanks for giving me TV set."

It is my pleasure. You will remember me each time, everyday, when you switch on TV set.

"I have neither forgotten you nor will forget throughout my life. I love you and continue that. I may not call you but do write you every fortnight."

That would be fine. At least I can read letter as many time as I wish. Each time I read imagine you are talking to me sitting by my side.

"All right darling good bye. Have a nice day."

Honey same to you. Bye.

I received her letters and read them peacefully. I read it number of time and feel she is talking to me.

One day I received a letter that she got job in the private hospital.

I was so cheerful and happy. I called and congratulate her.

"Thanks for the complements."

She gave me hospitals telephone number to call and talk to her.

I used to call her and talk longer time on this phone. I generally call her in the night time so that her job not to be disturbed.

"Why you spend too much on phone? Save money and come back quick."

Good suggestion. We were spending short duration on phone but still letters were continued. One day I was talking to her. She busted on telephone.

"There was only a Kasak left with me. I am regretful for that. It would be fulfilled or not only God knows."

What is that? I asked her.

"I told you earlier guess and recollect. If you are unable I tell you."

Tell me now. Time is running fast.

"A baby from you"

We both laughed on phone and line got disconnected.

One day I phoned hospital and came to know that she is admitted to cancer hospital.

I have no contact for that hospital. After a month I received a letter written by her brother along with his CV. He wrote that my sister is no more. She asked me to convey the message of her health to you and ask your help for myself. Therefore I am enclosing my CV if you can arrange some job for me would be great help.

I was upset. I did not take anything all the day. I pray God for peace of her soul and courage to her family to wear the pain due to her demise.

I took rose flower and offered her in the evening. I lit candle in the front of her photo. I pray God for her soul rest in the peace.

Really I know from her what love is. How people go mad in the love. Everything is possible in love. Passing a minute is not tolerable without her partner. Love is love even it last and rests on lust. Sex is biological requirement of the body. Human being can't live without this. It gives pleasure, joy and happiness to the person.

I was very much indulged with my wife in all her activities. She was happy and noticed remarkable changes in me. We respect each other and lead very happy life. Respect, love and many more unforgettable moments what we lived was remarkable. Hope future life will be peaceful.

Long live our love in thought and in heart.

END

THIS IS STORY OF A passionate, carving woman. She was in her mid thirty. She was so young to stay alone without her man. Sex is biological requirement of the body and soul without this people gets crazy. Desperate person can do anything. So she did what feel right at that time. She was happy as she got perfect companion for quenching her sexual desires.

Days were passing and their love affair was getting strong with time. They were quite happy and jolly person after this. They setup unforgettable love which was based on lust and faithful help. People were thinking them as couple though they were not.

She repents after wards but was too late. What happened was happened. Wave of time take away them in deep sea of love where they were swimming but could not get shore. They were enjoying the swimming of love, lust and pleasure while a tide of deadly disease came. She swept away in the deep sea and could not survive in the end.

He is thankful to her and offering a rose every evening to her in her memories. He could not forget her. Days and years were passed but her memories, act of love and enjoyment remain afresh in him.

The way he was trapped still put him bad situation when remembers that. He would have not accepted her proposal if family burden and responsibility back at home may not be there. Character less termination would be more painful than accepting this.

May God rest her sole in the peace!